NEW YORK REVIEW BOOKS
CLASSICS

T0244854

THE SUICIDES

ANTONIO DI BENEDETTO (1922–1986) was born in Mendoza, Argentina. He began his career as a journalist, writing for the Mendoza paper *Los Andes*. In 1953 he published his first book, a collection of short stories titled *Mundo animal*. He went on to write the novels *Zama*, *The Silentiary*, and *The Suicides* (all three published as NYRB Classics), which make up his Trilogy of Expectation; *Sombras, nada más*, his final novel, was published in 1985. Over the course of his career he received numerous honors, including a 1975 Guggenheim Fellowship and decorations from the French and Italian governments, and he earned the admiration of Jorge Luis Borges, Julio Cortázar, and Roberto Bolaño. In 1976, Di Benedetto was imprisoned and tortured by Argentina's military dictatorship; after his release in 1977 he went into exile in Spain. He returned to Buenos Aires in 1984, where he died less than two years later.

ESTHER ALLEN received the 2017 National Translation Award for her translation of Antonio Di Benedetto's *Zama*. A cofounder of the PEN World Voices Festival in New York City, she teaches at City University of New York's Graduate Center and Baruch College, where she directs the Sidney Harman Writer-in-Residence Program. Her work has been supported by fellowships from the Guggenheim Foundation, the National Endowment for the Arts, the Cullman Center for Scholars and Writers at the New York Public Library, and the Leon Levy Center for Biography. In 2006 the French government named her a Chevalier of the Order of Arts and Letters. Her essays, reviews, and translations have appeared in *The New York Review of Books*, *The Paris Review*, *Words Without Borders*, *Los Angeles Review of Books*, *Granta*, and other publications.

THE SUICIDES

ANTONIO DI BENEDETTO

Translated from the Spanish by
ESTHER ALLEN

NEW YORK REVIEW BOOKS

New York

THIS IS A NEW YORK REVIEW BOOK
PUBLISHED BY THE NEW YORK REVIEW OF BOOKS
207 East 32nd Street, New York, NY 10016
www.nyrb.com

Library of Congress Cataloging-in-Publication Data
Names: Di Benedetto, Antonio, 1922–1986, author. | Allen, Esther, 1962–
    translator.
Title: The suicides / by Antonio Di Benedetto; translated by Esther Allen.
Other titles: Suicidas. English
Description: New York: New York Review Books, 2025. | Series: New York
    Review Books classics
Identifiers: LCCN 2024003225 (print) | LCCN 2024003226 (ebook) | ISBN
    9781681378862 (paperback) | ISBN 9781681378879 (ebook)
Subjects: LCGFT: Novels.
Classification: LCC PQ7797.B4343 S813 2025 (print) | LCC PQ7797.B4343
    (ebook) | DDC 863/.64--dc23/eng/20240126
LC record available at https://lccn.loc.gov/2024003225
LC ebook record available at https://lccn.loc.gov/202400

ISBN 978-1-68137-886-2
Available as an electronic book; ISBN 978-1-68137-887-9

Printed in the United States of America on acid-free paper.
10 9 8 7 6 5 4 3 2 1

Tous les hommes sains ayant songé a leur propre suicide . . .

Todos los hombres sanos han pensado en su suicidio alguna vez.

Every sane man has thought about committing suicide at some point.

—Albert Camus

CONTENTS

First Part
DAYS WEIGHED DOWN WITH DEATH

MY FATHER took his life on a Friday afternoon.

He was thirty-three.

I'll be thirty-three the last Friday of next month.

Tía Constanza mentioned the coincidence, discreetly but tactlessly. I forgot all about it. Until today, when you might say it came looking for me.

At the agency, the boss said, "This could be your chance."

Without asking permission, he put three photos on my desk and explained my task: to figure out what he'd noticed about them.

"What do you see?"

I took it he was hoping for a display of some exceptional deductive prowess. Leaning forward, I scrutinized the photos. Each showed a human body, fully clothed, lying on the ground. "I see that all three are dead," I said.

"That's not a particularly clever response."

I could tell the biting tone was a warning. I needed to see better, and faster. I was annoyed but let it go; I must have sensed what I was starting to realize.

"One is a woman. The others are men," I observed.

I took stock very slowly, as if making a considerable effort to understand. I went on, in no hurry, "She and this guy here both have their eyes open. Unlike the third one."

5

The boss made a loud, impatient noise, turned, and started walking away.

I'm not exactly a comedian, I said to myself, and that was enough of that. Because he might decide that was enough, too.

I said, "The two with open eyes seem to be staring into…"

The boss stopped. I did, too.

I felt I'd understood something. And that what I understood mattered.

"They're staring… as if they were staring into themselves. But in horror."

I didn't need the grunt of approval he threw my way, or his subsequent silence, which gave the impression that one piece was still missing. Yes, there was a signal in my mind, a vague one. Until I declared, "They're terrified. There's terror in their eyes. But their mouths are grimacing in somber pleasure."

I didn't doubt I'd hit the mark and added something to his perception of the photos. That was done. The one thing I still needed to know, urgently, was my parting question.

"Were they murdered?"

"No. They killed themselves."

This was to be the embryo of a series of articles. A formless embryo.

We talked about the series. A story about the two cases with the terrified eyes. We don't know the story. Someone, a respectable person, a professional, provided the photos. This person can't help, won't tell us who these people are or who took the photos. Two cases aren't enough for a series. But we need their story. It will have to be investigated. Our own inquiry. The police won't work with us. We can try, but they won't. They don't release information on suicides. Publication can lead to contagion. Copycat suicides, an epidemic of suicides, a plague of suicides.

Why the introspective horror? Why the somber pleasure? On these points we'll offer some generalized conclusion to create more material for more articles, and for the whole series if we confirm the generalization. Yes: It can't just be the story of these two deaths, which are old news at this point. We need fresh cases. We'll have to wait. For what? For more of them to happen. To see. No, it can't wait, we've got two months, maximum. There's a circular prepared already, offering the series to the dailies. We can sell it to thirty evening papers and three magazines that do color. You want it sensationalized? No! Serious. Our agency doesn't sensationalize. Well, you said the evening papers . . . That was off the top of my head. For the magazines, you need color slides. Why are we only selling to the glossies? For the blood, so the red is visible. Otherwise it has to be marked with an arrow, explained in the caption: It gets lost. You're right. Work with Marcela. Why Marcela? Remember the piece on the plane crash in the mountains. She takes risks. There are no risks in this story, we're dealing with dead bodies here. Aren't there? Well, I hope not. Who knows.

I appeal: Pedro would be much better, I'd rather work with a man. No. Marcela. It's an order.

I don't say so, but I think of Marcela as something of an oddity. She's ascetic, or appears to be. She's new at the agency, I hardly know her. We don't like each other. I don't like her. I've let that be known. Someone asked why. I said "She's thirty or thirty-two." Years old, I meant.

I exit the building, relieved. Summer sunlight blinds me. It blinds me and soon leaves my whole body sticky.

Here, along the sidewalk, comes a blouse with a lot going on inside. I might have something to say to that. Here's another, cut low. I don't say anything this time, either, there's no use trying to start anything, they pass me by. But I do stare, and who knows what I look like because a middle-aged housewife is glaring at me reprovingly, trying to put me in my place.

I think about the series. I'll have to see people who are irrelevant to me because they're not the ones who did it— people who are forewarned, uncooperative. (Maybe Marcela will help me get through to them. In her own way, she's bait, thirty years old.)

I set my foot on the shoeshine block.

And I'll have to talk. To talk about it.

I think of Papá. I was like this boy here, the shoeshine boy, that size. I knew he'd died, but didn't know how. I cried until my tears dried up, then fell asleep, then woke up, as the ceremony continued, the visitors whispered. Someone, maybe my mother, was railing against "Unjust Death!" I understood the part about injustice—which left us without him—but I couldn't understand how Death crept into the house and took Papá. Because that morning he was alive, on his feet, as healthy as anybody else, and he died in the afternoon sunshine. And I thought Death was a sinister figure that dealt its blows in the dark of night.

What is death, I ask the boy shining my shoes.

He raises his brown eyes and considers me from below, surprised and intimidated, though he doesn't stop polishing.

The question was way too abstract. I change tack, and

smile, to connect with him. "Hasn't anybody you know ever died? A neighbor, an uncle..."

The boy bends down over his work, concentrating, then says, "Yes. Papá."

I say nothing.

He observes me covertly, with curiosity; I can see he's not rejecting me. I try—have I already started working on the piece?—to establish what he knows about the scope of death, where he thinks the person who dies is.

He answers that his father is in a niche. At first, his mother told him he'd gone on a trip. Now she says he's in Heaven. He doesn't believe it. He doesn't believe in Heaven? Yes, he believes in Heaven, but that's for good people, and his father used to hit his mother.

My day is weighed down with death. That's enough for now. I duck into a movie theater where *Alphaville* is playing. I'll work tomorrow.

Still, during the night, lying apart from Julia, though next to her, I think about what the shoeshine boy said and realize I never followed up on my initial question: What, for a child, is death?

I ask Julia to ask the students in her class about this. She's alarmed, bewildered, defensive. I explain, calm her down. The series, my work...

She refuses, obstinately. Says it's not normal.

"So then, I'm not normal?" I ask, to fluster her.

I know perfectly well that wasn't what she was saying.

*

I have breakfast with Mamá. It's a habit, the only time we ever spend together.

She tells me she ran into her friend Mercedes, and Doña Mercedes told her, "I have no family, only a TV set."

I object. "She has children and grandchildren. She lives with them."

"Yes, but they leave her by herself. They come and go, eat dinner with the TV on."

The reproach isn't directed at me, though I can deduce the moral of the story.

The heat, gradually invading the day, affects me. Mamá notices. She lowers the blinds, offers the electric fan.

I believe Mamá is the only person who loves me.

"I'd like to live in a country with snow," she says.

She's always said that. In response, I've offered to take her on a winter vacation. Each year I suggest it again.

"This year we'll go," I repeat.

"Where?"

"To the snow."

"Oh sí. Sí, *hijo*. We'll go."

Some mornings she's against the idea and tells me I need to save up for a little car. "You need it for your work."

This depresses me. Other people seem able to manage both: a car and snow.

My brother, who has a Fiat 1500, says, "Need a ride?"

Mamá knows her daily ration of this son of hers is over. She's sad about that, I can see, but my life is tied up in the streets.

My brother kisses his son and his daughter, and his second son, and his third son. The third is clutching a thoroughly mangled copy of issue 7 of *Minotauro*. I recognize it from what's left of the cover. I give him a slap and take it away.

From the kitchen door, my sister-in-law says, "Mauricio!"—
nothing more. She's sounding the alarm to her husband,
asking for help with that brother of his.

My brother exhibits restraint. He says, "Calm down."
Like a magistrate.

In the car, he doesn't speak.

Some idiot cuts us off but suffers no consequences because
Mauricio slams on the brakes just in time. He has every right
to yell but doesn't. I do.

I don't usually yell at anyone except on Saturdays.

Marcela has the late-afternoon shift. I won't be able to see
her until four o'clock. I'm sure she doesn't yet know she'll
be working with me.

Aceituno, the agency reporter assigned to police head-
quarters, can't link the photos to any story he's worked on.
He circulates them in the reporters' room and they come
back around without having struck a chord in the experts'
memories.

Aceituno takes me to Forensics and leaves me with the
chief of the unit.

I ask the chief to work with us on some information, for
the agency. The agency can have all the information it wants,
unless it has to do with a case a judge is about to rule on, a
crime under special investigation, pedophilia, or suicide.

I haven't mentioned the photos yet. I'm going to act as if
I don't know they fall into one of the off-limits categories.

Do I have time to see the in-house museum? Yes, I do.
What matters, in the end, is the elbow-rubbing.

We drink some coffee next to the severed head of a ma-
fioso with three bullet holes in his face. It's been in a glass

case for thirty years. A special formula preserves the skin color.

He speaks of "judicial corpses" and I lay out the problem. If I'm in possession of a photograph of a judicial corpse—that is, a corpse found in circumstances that require the intervention of the police and the judiciary—but I don't have a name or any other information, how can it be identified?

He mentions the missing persons archive, the protocols observed for all bodies that undergo an autopsy, the technicians' visual memory, specific features that can narrow the field by revealing the gender, approximate age, season when the person died (by the clothing), surroundings they died in, and much more.

"Then it is possible?"

"Absolutely possible."

At that, I pull out the photos and ask for identifications and histories.

He picks them up, looks at them, sets them down, and says, "These look like suicides."

"They *are* suicides."

He says, "Absolutely impossible."

On our way out we go through the labs. There's a girl in a white coat with very pale skin. She notices me. That's something, at least.

I walk for a bit, looking for a restaurant with two characteristics: grilled fish and people I don't know, who won't talk to me about things I am fully aware of because they're in all the newspapers and our opinions on them are formed by all the same magazines.

A tourist standing next to me as I look at a menu in a

window asks where he can try some of the local cuisine. Then he changes his mind—maybe he guessed what I was thinking of for my lunch—and asks for directions to the aquarium. As he heads off, he thanks me, saying, "You people have a very nice city here." To this compliment, I reply that he can't say "you people" because I don't have anything; the city doesn't belong to me. He says, "Oh, you're not from here either." We may not have understood each other.

It's the season. There are many tourists around and the lady tourists give everyone a lot to look at, which is exactly what they want, which is all very nice.

In fact, last night, again, I dreamed I was walking around naked.

At the agency I show the photos to the woman in charge of the archives. From long professional habit, her first impulse isn't to look at them but to turn them over and look for the registry number and date of receipt or publication. There's nothing there.

"These aren't ours," she lets me know, unnecessarily.

"Do you remember them, for any reason? Do they remind you of anything?"

Now she's enjoying them.

"They're fantastic!" she exclaims. She wants to know more. "Who are they? What happened to her? Raped?"

Next I pay a visit to Bibi, who's busy ransacking a Polish magazine written in English. She's the agency translator and for that reason, as well as for her unfailing and perfectly ordered memory, we call her Fichero—Card Catalogue.

I pull a chair over to the table where she's sitting and do my best to appear friendly, starting with my face.

"May I trouble you for some assistance?"

Other people address her as *tú*, as if on intimate terms. But I use the formal *usted* when asking for her help. It's not as if I'm currently "with" her. We don't play the same sports, either, and I don't spend all day kidding around, like the rest of them do.

"What's this about?"

"Suicide."

"Whose?"

"Wish I knew... Not mine, at least."

"Ah sí." Card Catalogue is off and running. "The Melanesian who threw himself out of a palm tree, and number 350 who jumped off the Eiffel Tower on March 12, 1967. Demosthenes and Marilyn Monroe, Stefan Zweig and his wife, Werther and Kirilov, Anna Karenina, Sappho, and the Mundugumor who sacrifices himself by going alone to the enemy island where the cannibal tribe will eat him. That kind of thing?"

"Exactly that kind of thing."

"And also: 1963 in Vietnam, Buddhist monks in yellow robes, gasoline and a match; the unemployed warrior's hara-kiri with a wooden sword—poor guy, there's no war. And the gas oven for the housewife who doesn't believe the doctor and knows that her stomachache is cancer. That too?"

"That too. And this." I put the photos down in front of her.

Bibi takes a long look but it's obvious she isn't getting clear on much. I try to orient her with a quick summary so she can suggest where I should begin, at least as far as resolving the two cases goes. The Melanesia part will come in later.

Still, she's working the problem, wants to know more about what we might glean from Forensics. I repeat that there's no collaborating with them. "I have a friend," Bibi tells me, and at that moment, Marcela enters silently and waits. Bibi makes a date with me. "Tomorrow night, at the bowling alley."

I take the photos back from her, hand them to Marcela, and say "*Vamos.*"

I usher her downstairs to the café. While we're in the elevator she's studying the woman sprawled on her back.

We sit down and I place the photos on the table, facing me. She watches and waits, very serious. She has yet to greet me or say a single word.

I ask whether she knows what we've gotten ourselves into. A gesture: More or less.

As she examines one of them, she looks fresh (as if she'd just showered) and poised, and seems more acceptable. She's not doing anything that makes me want to find fault with her.

I ask whether she'd be able to photograph a quake.

She says yes. To make sure she grasps my meaning, I clarify, "An earthquake," demonstrating the shaking with my hands.

She says yes again, seemingly undaunted by the challenge.

I insist. "The quake itself, not its effects and consequences: not people running or a collapsing wall or a toppled church spire."

She confirms that she can, and I ask what she did during Monday's earthquake. Did she take photos?

"I slept. Had no idea it was happening. I thought somebody was moving the bed."

"Who could be moving your bed?" I inquire, maliciously.

"An earthquake," she answers, with no sign of annoyance.

Is she steamrolling me because I tried to shock her? In any case, I explain that the job we have to do—the series—"will be easier because the subjects are all prone and still."

She nods. "Yes."

She points questioningly at the woman's contradictory expression.

I explain that that's our pretext. When she asks whether I chose to work with her, I say I don't often take much initiative, but she does.

She says they don't leave her time for that, they give orders and there's always lots to do.

I ask what she'd like to be taking pictures of if she had extra time and film and she answers, "Purity." I point out that purity is as fleeting and abstract as an earthquake.

She says, and people's backs, too, because that's what they're most careless of, everyone thinks we only see what they want us to see—the carefully made-up eyes, the mustache, the Italian necktie, the expression of intelligence. I say that to my mind the back of the body is the least expressive part, and she agrees, and that it would be like taking photos of people who are fast asleep, though it's probably not easy to sneak into bedrooms, especially when two people are sleeping together. Anyway, if what she wants is people who don't care that they're being photographed, she'll have the ones in the series. And there, I tell her, we arrive back at something she may not like much, and I clarify that I didn't request her for this job. I add, though there's no need, that that doesn't prevent us from working together.

Since she has no reaction to my polite acknowledgment, I tell her our first step is to figure out who the two faces belonged to. From the police we can expect nothing and our colleagues have said they don't remember anything.

I ask her to make copies of the photos and tell her we're going to show them to everybody, "the waiter, the three aviators, Jean-Louis Trintignant and Anouk Aimée, my tía Constanza, Carlos Gardel, Marcela's boyfriend."

She shoots me a warning glance.

I think I did it on purpose, the mention of a boyfriend, to see if she has one. I'm going to be working with her for two months, who knows what might happen . . .

Half an hour later I'm watching *Omicron: The Fiery Creature from Planet Ultra*.

Afterward I meet up with Julia.

She greets me with a sheaf of pages torn from school notebooks that she flings at me as if to separate herself from contact with them.

I glimpse what this is about and feign surprise, adopting an expression of tender reconciliation as I gather up the pages without looking at them. It doesn't work. She's boiling over.

I let her indulge in her anger and pick up the top page. "Topic: Death." I rifle through the rest. The handwriting changes, the topic remains the same.

I read: "Bobby's death. I cried a lot, a lot. We buried him under a tree and I take him food and water."

(No mention of who Bobby was, but it must have been the family dog, and the student imagines he's still alive or some part of him is.)

Another: "A truck had its wheel stuck in the acequia. The man with the iron bar was working hard to lift the axle. He let go of the lever, took a few steps back, fell backward as if he were sitting down into a chair, and stayed like that with his back against the wall. He was very pale and they told us to get away from there."

(This one has no concept of death but recognizes the sight of a dead man.)

Another: "The *padre cura* says there are three kinds of dead people: those in Paradise, those in Purgatory, and those in Hell, where it's very hot, even more than here in summertime and more than in Africa. I think I'm going to like Paradise: It's like recess. It would also be nice if it were like Africa and there were a pool to swim in."

Another: "Death must be a lady who lives near my house. She has a lot of filthy cats. She's old, she's dirty, and she's bad. That's why she lives alone. Nobody loves her."

(Death is a person.)

Disappointed, I stop reading. Still, I'm rather grateful and say, "You decided to help me—"

"I'll lose my job! When the inspector sees what I asked them to write."

I'm annoyed. "Why would he have to see this?'

I look back down at the stack of papers and read: "Rosita's brother, who was in high school, was sick, and died. During siesta, Rosita called and asked if I wanted to see him. I wanted to but said what if they see us? She said there's nobody here, it's hot. We stood on a chair and looked at him through the glass he had over his face. I think he was sleeping. This is a secret between Rosita and me."

(Sees death as akin to sleep.)

Julia sighs. I pause. This is a warning: If I don't start paying attention to her she'll start crying. But she shouldn't claim to be my victim. I won't let her rub my face in what she did. I'd rather explain to her about last night. Maybe persuade her to see things my way.

"Men," I tell her, "want the woman to obey. They have bosses, the business owners who order them around all day. They come home and need to vent; they want to be the one in charge for a change. I obey. I have bosses. I answer to an owner. Even so, I'm not interested in having anyone obey me. I don't expect that. When I asked you to help me, with your kids at school, I didn't mean to give you an order... Come on, don't contradict me. Other times, yes; this time, no."

"Why not this time?" And, despite everything, she's sobbing.

I hesitate, I don't let her pain upset me, I take my time. After a while I say, "Because apparently I have a passionate interest in this question."

(Though, in general, I never feel passionate about anything.)

Julia, seeing herself displaced once more, gives up. "That's enough for today."

She leaves. I make no move to stop her.

She's forgotten the pages from the school notebooks.

I read: "My little brother, el Bebe, killed himself. I loved him very much but I don't miss him because he didn't know how to talk or walk or anything even though he was almost six months old. He and my other brother, the one that's alive, were born together, they were twins. My mamá says she usually nursed one of them first and then the other, and the first is the one who survived because she put him on the left side. When it was the other one's turn, el Bebe's, he didn't want to suck and he stopped drinking milk and died of starvation. That was because she didn't attend to him first, my mamá says, but when she figured it out it was too late.

The doctor said el Bebe committed suicide and Papá said it was a big disgrace, but that he was used to it, other people in the family had killed themselves, too. I heard them saying this, they didn't tell me."

My mother has left a plate for me in the kitchen.

I eat dinner. Everything is clean, the silence is wondrous, I feel at ease. Living is good sometimes.

I go into the dining room for another bottle of wine. I switch on the light and find myself face-to-face with Papá, in his portrait.

In his portrait, he's forever young. He'll never be old.

No one can ever humiliate him.

If you're not alive, you don't have to endure having anyone else allow you to live. Other people allow us to live but they dictate how.

Will I be old? Will I stand on a sidewalk someday in a long line of retirees?

Do you have to wait for death, like an elderly retiree, or do you have to *do it*, the way Papá did?

I uncork the bottle and death becomes a person for me, as if I were a small child. And not an old woman with mangy cats, either. She's like Mae West. A little old-fashioned, I mean, and plump and sensual, legs crossed, perched on a bench, smoking, next to the bar. She waits. She's waiting for us.

I pour her a glass of my red wine.

I feel a hand touching mine. It's Mamá's gentle way of waking me up without startling me.

"A young lady is looking for you, from the agency."

I yawn.

"A young lady? What's she like?"

"She has a Beetle."

Marcela and her Citroën. I jump out of bed. She's come up with something.

"Invite her in."

"I did. She's in the living room but doesn't want to sit down. She's in a rush, says to tell you there's a case."

I skip breakfast but have some black coffee in the kitchen. The glass of red wine I served Mae West is still there.

It happened up in the hills, which means an hour's drive and a good chance of arriving after it's all been cleaned up. Two students killed themselves. Either one killed the other and then himself, or each did it on his own, though together.

Marcela found out in a newsroom. She was going from paper to paper with the photos, exploiting friendships. And encountering no memory of the two cases among any reporters on the police beat.

I tell her the story of el Bebé. She finds it reasonable. "The mother had passed him over."

I believe the story and agree with the schoolboy who thought it was a suicide. But I say the opposite, to provoke Marcela.

She doesn't react.

I insist. "A suicide? In the cradle? Not plausible."

She won't be drawn into an argument. She simply shares a conviction. "We're born with death inside us."

I fall back on Mae West. "Death waits outside us."

She doesn't reply and I don't go on because I decide it's nothing but a word game. She said "inside," I said "outside."

The feebleness of my reply annoys me but has exhausted my line of argument, though I wanted to express something that had meaning, a meaning that escapes me. I analyze myself and recognize that I'm a void.

The sun has claimed the bare, treeless hills for itself, pounding them with its fire and splendor. The roadway ascends and from a high point we can see the group of cars.

Marcela is taking out her equipment when a police officer's rigid index finger moves back and forth to say "No photos." We protest, to no avail. We can enter the area only if Marcela leaves the camera behind in the car.

The bodies are already on stretchers but the stretchers are still on the ground. They're both covered by rough tarps.

I want to see the faces. The police won't let me approach. I appeal: "Where's the judge?" An older man walks over, the sort who inspires respect on sight. I'm not sure whether it's his bearing or, on this occasion, his air of deep gravity. He asks if he can be of service and says, "I'm the father."

He's barely glanced at me but I notice he gives Marcela a quick, penetrating once-over.

The father speaks to another man, the court clerk. The judge hasn't come; the clerk is in charge.

For our benefit, he'll ask them to uncover the head of one of the dead boys. The eyelids have fallen shut, depriving me of the expression in the eyes. There's blood and dirt on the mouth, but no grimace. I'd imagined the bullet going in at the temple, but that's not the case. I ask where the bullet hole is.

"This young man was killed by the other one."

The policeman lifts the tarp higher; the shirt is torn, there are powder burns and splotches of red on the chest.

We move to the second boy, who committed murder, then killed himself.

His eyes aren't open either. I need to ask a question. But who do I ask?

The father is standing next to us, or, rather, next to Marcela. She consults him discreetly. "Your son?"

He nods gravely.

I should ask how long ago it happened, when they found out about it, and when the father (who strikes me as far more intrigued by Marcela's proximity than sorrowed by the death of his offspring) arrived on the scene. I ask, instead, "Did they find him like this, with the eyes closed? Was he just the way he is now?"

"No, señor, I myself…" and he stretches out toward me the hand that closed the eyelids.

"Can you tell me what his gaze revealed?"

He's losing control, doesn't know how to react. I come to his aid. "Some kind of emotion, señor, some kind of pain. Sorrow, fear, pride, pleasure—what?"

"Fear? No, señor. My son was not afraid. You can see that. A grown man doesn't do what he did. Fear? My son? No, no señor. There was nothing in his eyes. My word as a gentleman: I saw nothing, nothing."

He's growing vehement. And has fixated on one word: fear. Why?

Since this one's not giving me anything, maybe the other one's father will. But I can't figure out who that might be.

What's more, they're already picking up the stretchers. Marcela whispers, "Let's go with them." "For what?" I say, and she says, "You have to cover me." The suicide's father proves to have good ears and to be a quicker study than I am.

He tells her calmly, "Come along with me, they'll be less suspicious."

I let them go on ahead. I'd rather distract the police officer and the court clerk, who are walking together.

"Where's the other boy's family?"

"We sent a message. We don't know if it got to them and we can't wait any longer. This heat, the flies..."

Yes, the flies. They're also settling on me.

There's a pause, and in the sudden silence the words of one stretcher-bearer to another can distinctly be heard: "Beautiful day, isn't it?"

He says it with conviction. As he walks, bearing the weight of his cargo, he gazes around the best he can at the firmament, so blue and diaphanous. Perhaps he smells the grass and thinks about the foxes and partridges he could be hunting, and about the meat he'll grill and the matés he'll sip at day's end.

Beautiful day, yes. Not for the boys. They deprived themselves of it.

"Why'd they do it? Things weren't working out between them?"

The police officer: "What things?"

"Come on, you know."

The court clerk: "I think it was a pact. That's my intuition."

"A pact?"

"A pact: when two people agree to kill themselves."

In case one of them loses their nerve, or because they've realized they share the same motive. Who knows.

On the trip back we form a caravan along the narrow dirt road. We're the last car, and the dust cloud makes for a challenging drive.

Marcela isn't saying anything so I ask if she managed to get some good shots.

"I won't know until I develop the film. I couldn't focus."

She shows me a miniature camera, and I take it from her for a closer look. Anyone would think it was a toy.

"The old man went along with it," I say.

"He's not an old man."

"I think he was happiest talking to you."

"Perfectly natural. I was the only woman there and he needed emotional support."

"He told you that?"

"No. I sensed it."

"I think he'd like to see you again, just the two of you next time."

"He wants to see the photos. He'll call me."

She knows why he'll call—certainly not for the photos—and she didn't refuse to give him her number. Is Marcela available? That would be unusual, there's no woman without a man. They all have someone lined up, always. Marcela may be taking a break right now or looking for someone new. If that's the case, why the old man and not me?

I feel a twinge of excitement, but the Citroën is full of dust and I'm caked with it in this heat.

Tomorrow.

At the bowling alley, Bibi's in the middle of a game with some guy. I make sure she knows I'm there, but I don't interrupt and she doesn't stop playing.

I stay in the bar, at the barren bar's bar.

Behind me, the bowling alley echoes like a deep canyon. The sound of the balls striking the pins isn't unpleasant. I think of drumsticks, dried-out hollow tree trunks, Indians, carpentry, planks being unloaded, twelve colored pencils rolling out of their case, the schoolteacher's pen tapping against her desk, a baton, Toscanini clicking two batons against each other in midair, firewood collapsing as it burns, carbon, the black hair on the back of a Black man's neck (Cassius Clay), knockout.

She comes in. Of course, it had to be her.

It's Piel Blanca, the pale-skinned woman from Forensics, and she's looking for Bibi, who's nearby.

Bibi hands her a pair of special shoes designed for bowling. They seem better suited to basketball or boxing. Piel Blanca takes her shoes off and puts them away in her purse, a rather dirty thing to do. She takes over for the guy. The guy kisses Bibi on the cheek, a friend's kiss, and moves out of sight.

I'm still at the bar. Barre, bear, bier. I order a beer.

Piel Blanca leans forward to release the ball. Her body reveals itself, excites me.

Exactly forty-seven minutes later we're all sitting at a small round table.

Piel Blanca's name turns out, in fact, to be Blanca. Bibi calls her Blanquita.

Forensics won't cooperate. What's the goal here, precisely? To identify two suicides. What do we have to go on? Some photos. Do you have them here? They're quite dramatic. What else have you got? Nothing. What more do you need? Nothing more? Yes: the story. To publish it? I don't know... What for, then? I have to figure something out. Do I have to say it? If you want to... Why that face, why those eyes, why that mouth. Well, because they killed themselves. But isn't it strange? Yes. Why does it seem strange to you, too? I can't figure it out. Pleasure and fear. Have you seen this in any others? To be honest, I haven't looked for it. But I wasn't looking for it in these either. If you hadn't said anything...

Piel Blanca will cooperate.

When we say goodbye to her outside, leaving her to wait for a bus, I ask Bibi, "Why is she taking the risk?"

What I really want to know is whether she's expecting to be paid, but that must not have occurred to either woman because Bibi grows annoyed. "Didn't I tell you we're friends? Or do you think she's doing it for you?"

She hesitates a second, then completes the thought. "You're quite an unpleasant individual, you know."

I defy expectations by acknowledging her point, which confounds her and causes her to take it back. After a few moments of shared silence, she says, "I have my 4L parked around the corner. Can I drop you somewhere?"

I accept the offer. I'll go see Julia.

As I'm getting out of the car, Bibi says, "Just a moment," rummages around in her purse, and hands me a slip of paper. She apologizes—"I'd forgotten about this"—and pulls away.

I read:

A twenty-six-year-old man succumbs to melancholy and throws himself from the roof of his house. A brother, who was caring for him, reproaches himself for the death, makes several attempts at suicide, and dies a year later after prolonged and repeated episodes of self-starvation. Another brother of these two men, who two years earlier had declared in terrifying despair that he would not escape their fate, also kills himself. (Jean-Étienne Esquirol, cited to the best of my ability.)

What is this...?

My brother killed himself at age sixty. I had never thought about it seriously, but when I reached fifty, the memory came back to me more vividly and now it never leaves me. (A patient, to Alexandre Brière de Boismont.)

What is this...?
"A twenty-six-year-old man succumbs to melancholy..." "Esquirol, cited to the best of my ability." Oh, right: Card Catalogue.

"You've destroyed my life. This time you truly have destroyed my life. Oh, why did I ever meet you?"

Julia's wondering why she ever met me and I'm wondering why I ever came to see her. "I'm leaving," I say.

Then she really loses her temper, making me suspect I haven't destroyed her yet and she's exaggerating, to get something out of me. But what? I ask, in a kindly tone, what it is that she wants from me, and this moment of sunshine moves her. Even so, she pretends to shut me out.

"Nothing. Not anymore."

I point out that saying she doesn't want anything anymore must mean she once expected something from me that I haven't been able to give her.

She says, "I've given you my life."

This seems exaggerated, too, but I go along with it. "Yes."

Now she exclaims, "Oh! All I want is for you to love me, truly, just a little bit."

"I do love you—"

"I know, I know, but I want you to love me a little more."

I say all right and give her a kiss. She calms down.

"Did I really destroy your life? Did something happen today?"

"One of the kids, Clota Barbuján, went home and told her parents I made them write about death. Her father came to school to talk to the principal."

"What did the principal say?"

"He's afraid. He says Dr. Barbuján is very influential."

"What will you do?"

"Defend myself. But the principal wanted to see the kids' homework and I didn't have it. You took it."

"I didn't take it. You gave it to me, you threw it at me, you forgot about it. How was I supposed to know what you intended to do with it?"

"You could have given it back, you could have brought it with you just now. I said I took it home to go over it but that excuse is only good until tomorrow."

I say, "I know Barbuján. I'm going to have to go knock some sense into him."

Now I'm the one who's exaggerating. I feel like doing it, I really do, but I won't.

Julia takes me seriously and grows alarmed: "No, no. Don't have anything to do with him. And don't even think about the principal. You'll only cause more trouble for me."

You'll cause trouble for me. What a perfect egotist. Though, of course, she's right to be one.

I take a taxi home and return with the stack of pages.

"Will I see you tomorrow?"

"No. It's Saturday."

Why does she ask? She knows. Saturday means boxing.

*

I tuck into my dinner long after midnight and without much appetite. But I don't ignore it because it would pain my mother to find the dishes she prepared for me untouched.

I reread the notes that Bibi the Card Catalogue gave me.

"Another brother...who two years earlier had declared in terrifying despair that he would not escape their fate, also kills himself."

"My brother killed himself at age sixty. I had never thought about it seriously, but when I reached fifty, the memory came back to me more vividly and now it never leaves me."

I realize only a few words would have to change.

"My father killed himself at thirty-three. I had never thought about it seriously but as I began approaching that age, the memory came back to me more vividly..."

Up to that point, in fact, it fits. But not the ending: "and now it never leaves me."

I'm aware that I'm protecting myself by pretending that I don't think about it constantly. And at the same time, distant scenes filter into my memory, scenes that are predominantly visual.

First, I'm walking through a special place—a sanatorium —with my father. I don't see him. I don't remember what he looked like then. I feel his hand, a man's hand, and my own hand, a child's, entrusted to his.

Then his hand has left me. I find myself in the sanatorium's courtyard surrounded by tiled walls. I'm on a strange, circular, sky-blue wicker bench, with a planter in the middle.

Later I get up from the bench. (I've grown tired of waiting, Papá's not coming back, I'm a little afraid of this place.) I walk toward the room I watched him go into. It's summer and the door is wide open. I reach the threshold and stop. There's a bed, and Papá is next to it. In the bed lies Paolo, his face tilted up, his head against a high mound of pillows. His eyes are closed. He has trouble breathing.

(Paolo is my cousin, my oldest cousin. He fired a shotgun into his stomach.)

I have a dream about my English professor, a woman.

(I have no English professor.)

Over breakfast, I ask my mother to tell me more about certain vague images that, until now, were packed away deep in my childhood.

Alongside them, I have others that no one in any family gathering has ever alluded to in my presence, which is why I've come to doubt their authenticity or at least the accuracy of my memory.

Here are the scenes I will not resurrect with my mother: My paternal grandfather, his peasant build, heavy clothes, goatee, and tall, straight cane, not for support but as a symbol of command, of war. His pleasure in taking me for a stroll through the vineyards, his way of pausing, picking some fruit from the vine, conversing. And his need to pour into my soul, with stern bitterness, his unfortunate childhood, his life of hard work. Then, voice charged with passion, he would chaotically evoke distant chapters of our family history and the source of the special pride he took in them: the bravery and daring of our forebearers—his and mine both, he specified—who were soldiers or suicides. Then he would proclaim in his Italian dialect that I understood perfectly, "Twelve—twelve suicides there have been among us."

Were these fantasies of glory, the revenge of a man whose life had been filled with humiliation and adversity? Did he dream this history? Did I dream he dreamed it?

If it wasn't a dream, then counting my father, who wasn't tallied in my grandfather's count, the number of suicides added up to thirteen.

Even setting aside the high numbers my grandfather exalted, isn't it the case that during my own lifetime two of my relatives have put an end to themselves?

There's only one, the older cousin, gasping for air on his pillow, that I can ask my mother about, though it's certain to distress her. She's slow to respond, perhaps thinking that if she can put me off this once I won't insist again. "There's so much I have to do this morning: the shopping, soup for the children."

She keeps stalling. "We're in the middle of breakfast... is this the right time to talk about sad things?"

It's true, the hour of coffee and buttered toast is not a melancholy time, as the sun makes the kitchen its own and happily colors the air.

I don't push her, but she senses my anxiety and reluctantly gives in. "I was almost twenty... Grandfather had just come back from Italy, where he went to look for grapevines that would be hardier, more resistant to disease. Here's the story: He brought back some vines and also a widow, a very young widow. She'd be useful, he said, for working the land. Those were different times, desperate people were easy to come by. They fled here from Europe so they could eat.

"Your cousin Paolo fell in love with the widow. And she? What can I tell you: She adored him. But they had to hide from everyone, especially Grandfather, as you can imagine. We all knew that if he found out what was going on something terrible would happen.

"One night when I was feeling very lonely because you'd stayed in the city with your father, what we'd all been dread-ing happened. Grandfather realized the widow wasn't in his bed, and then, naturally, began to understand. He went straight to Paolo's room and found the door locked. He tried to force it open as his voice got louder and louder, that voice of his that shook us all to the core. He ordered them to open the door, he cursed, he pounded it with his cane and his feet. The door shivered, the house trembled. Everyone was awake but none of us dared leave our rooms.

"The old man became an animal, a madman. He kept screaming a filthy word at the widow, screaming at the boy that he was going to kill him.

"Half an hour went by, *hijo*, at least half an hour. I was sick with terror...

"We heard a shot...

"Grandfather fell silent, at last.

"We began to appear one by one in the hallway, barefoot, without putting our clothes on. After all the noise, a silence had fallen, such a heavy silence...

"We heard someone inside lift the latch. The door swung open and the widow raised a lamp so we could see what was in there and do something. Paolo was lying on the floor, curled in a ball, unconscious, wearing only his shirt. He had the hunting rifle between his legs. A bloodstain was spreading across his shirt..."

I walk past Bibi's office, acting casual. With feigned indifference, I wonder out loud: Was she trying to suggest, in the notes she gave me, that suicide is a hereditary disease?

"No!" she replies in surprise. "No conclusion whatsoever. It's only two cases and they're very old, but representative. In case they were useful to you. I wanted to help."

Now she's calling me *tú*, as if we were on intimate terms. Well, well ...

Will we keep working on the story of the two students? I'm not so sure, but we don't have anything else today. It's Saturday and the courts are closed, Marcela warns. I explain that I have the clerk's private phone number. She tells me to call and I do and he's there. He'll work with us.

He says he searched the bedroom of the one who shot a bullet into his friend before killing himself.

He gives me the lay of the land—"Family has lots of money, eh"—then specifies, "He didn't leave a note, not even for his parents. But I found a notebook with a story. My theory is confirmed: It was a pact. The judge will be satisfied. On Monday I'll give him my work, almost complete."

"Can I see the notebook?"

He says I can't, then agrees to let me leaf through it, though he imposes strict constraints.

I tell Marcela we should go. She says, "Not me."

"Why?" Why is she jumping ship now? Her gesture says it's not worth it.

It's true, this thing, the case of the two boys isn't the main question, and on the main question I've made no progress.

It's true, I say to myself, this thing—the series—isn't worth the trouble. I can get out of it, though I foresee some trouble retaining my job if I do.

The phone. It's Julia. She says, "It's horrible."

"I don't want to know about anything horrible," I say and hang up.

Marcela overhears and shoots me a curious look. She's smoking, with her legs crossed. She's not thirty. She's much younger.

The phone again. I ignore it. It rings and rings. Marcela picks up. She covers the receiver with one hand and says, "It's for you... a woman."

Something in my brain is shooting out sparks. I bury my head, defeated. But manage not to moan.

I can hear Marcela explaining. "I don't know where he went... or if he's coming back."

The boss shows up. He tries to revive me. "What gives?" He guesses, "You two are quarreling?" Marcela shakes her head. In such cases, the woman's testimony is enough. The boss completely forgets that we have our own private lives.

"There was a case yesterday, two students. You let it get away."

"No, we didn't," Marcela steps in on my behalf. "We've got it. We were there."

"Where's the material, then? I haven't seen anything."

"We're cooking something up," says Marcela. "For the series."

"Oh... but it was news. The other papers had it."

"It's our understanding that the news is always Aceituno's job."

"He came down with something and didn't come in."

I speak up. "You'll have the full story by evening. A scoop."

"This evening will be too late," he protests, but leaves without saying he won't accept the story, meaning that he's tempted by the scoop.

"Now I have to see the notebook," I tell Marcela.

"Five o'clock," I add. That's when she needs to have the photos ready for me. Understood. I sense that the interest she felt a few moments ago has vanished. I consult her. "Shall I break up with her?" "It's not worth it." "What's not worth it?" "Judging whether something's bad or good. Nothing is bad, if it's necessary." Saying this is her way of forgiving me, I think.

It's a notebook with soft covers. I read the first part.

"We were in chemistry class and the teacher was writing out the lesson on the board but I told myself I was somewhere else and didn't copy down the formulas.

"I tore out a page and wrote, 'I am going to kill myself.'

"I sat still for a while, as if I were empty. I realized I'd reached a point I'd been preparing for.

"I felt a chill and examined my soul to see if it was fear and couldn't determine whether it was. Then I realized it could also be pleasure.

"At that moment, something unexpected came over me, an attack of vanity, I guess, and I rolled the paper up into a little tube and slipped it onto Manuel's desk, the way we sometimes do to help each other out during exams.

"Manuel checked to be sure the teacher's back was turned. He unrolled it and I felt his gaze, deeply questioning.

"I watched as he, in turn, added a few words to the same paper and slipped it back to me.

"After my words, 'I am going to kill myself,' he'd written, 'Me, too.'

"I was offended. It felt as if Manuel was cheapening my action. He didn't believe me, and was only making fun of me with his idle boast that he, too, could also 'kill himself' just like me.

"It was a provocation and I dug in my heels. I decided to make him commit to it, scare him so badly he'd be forced to back down. The dialogue continued, the paper coming and going between us:

"'Then what are you waiting for?'

"'Nothing.'

"'When?'

"'I haven't thought about it.'

"'When you're 177 years and 7 months old?'

"This time it took a long while for the paper to come back. I looked over at Manuel. Until then both of us had been pretending to follow the lesson, our eyes on the bit of chalk in the teacher's fingers. Manuel's face had an expression of sincere joylessness.

"Still, I decided to back him into a corner. On another piece of paper I scribbled, 'Would you do it right now, in the bathroom, with a noose?'

"When it reached him, he unrolled it on his desk and I understood that the time for quick replies was over. Manuel was meditating and I felt certain of my superiority.

"A few minutes went by before he picked up the pen again; when he did it was to ask me a question: would I really do it. With energy, I wrote down, 'Yes, I will do it,' and emphatically underscored the words.

"'Why?' he wanted to know.

"'And why not?' I replied."

At that point the story pauses and there's a blank space on the page. The suspension is timely: That magnetic final line has captivated me.

Indeed. The question isn't why I would kill myself. It's why I wouldn't kill myself.

The court clerk offers me a cup of coffee, I'm in his home. Without looking at him, I say, "Just a moment," underscoring the words with a gesture. Immediately I'm aware of my own insolence. I'd practically shooed him away—"Don't interrupt, don't be a nuisance"—when there was no need for that at all.

I go on reading.

They talked about it many times after that, until they set a date, which the notebook records. (I check; they stuck to their plan.)

From that point on they tried to do things they hadn't done before: sweat in a Turkish bath, shoplift, burn down a tree, sell newspapers at dawn, bet on a racehorse, cut a rooster's head off, kill their fathers.

Each killed his own father symbolically. The one writing the diary made a sketch of his father, naked, with all his attributes, then scribbled out the genitals and made a circle over the heart like the mouth of a hole. The other one gradually stole all his father's belts, one by one, and cut them into little pieces. He called the belts "torturers."

They decided on a method for killing themselves, after much reflection, discussion, reading, and speculation. They chose a gun, for speed. They stole it from the torturer father. Days before, they carried it off for a few hours to rehearse, "to listen to it," says the notebook. They went, as they would again in the end, to the solitude of the hills. The first to fire, against himself, would be the one who drew the short straw. Then the gun would be left for the second one, who would use it immediately. They hated the idea of disfigurement, wanted a bullet to the chest. (I compare this to the facts of the case: They didn't carry it out as they'd planned. Why? When the moment arrived, did Manuel lose his courage, and then his friend "had" to kill him?)

They said goodbye to a number of things and to hardly any people. The author of the notebook tormented himself trying to choose the right words to say goodbye to his mother without rousing her suspicions. "I wanted to give her a kiss but I haven't done that for so long it might make her wonder." Many times, with slight variations, he wrote, "I'll get up from the table before they do. I'll say 'See you tomorrow,' and gaze at them from the doorway." Once he added, "If they only knew…"

"If they only knew…" The sweetness of it is like a hope of being saved.

When she sees me, Mamá starts worrying. "Has something happened?"

I smile. "I came for lunch."

Mamá sighs in relief but is still worried. "If only you'd said so. Will you be all right with the food all the rest of us have? You're never here weekdays, only on Sundays, certain Sundays."

At the table, my sister-in-law tries to demonstrate that she's no longer upset with me for having scolded her son. Loudly enough to be overhead, as if making a joke, she says to her husband, with a sidelong glance, in a protective and affectionate tone, "He looks like a normal person."

The effect is as intended. Without needing to speak I demonstrate that everything's fine. Because really, it's all the same to me.

Am I a normal man? I don't make much noise. I like many things. I live my life. I wonder why we are alive.

I think about death, I resist it, I prefer to live. But I think about it.

Many people don't. They take it for granted that a great deal of future remains to them.

At the table, the silverware is doing its work. Mine too. Mamá is on the alert, keeping an eye on me.

I feel quite down, and it's very hot.

After lunch I have a siesta.

I wake up at twenty to five. I don't think I'll turn the story in. Marcela will be waiting for me with the photos. She'll get tired, she'll leave. Though I could let her know.

I'd rather go to the movies. There's no sci-fi anywhere so I see *Doctor Zhivago*. Zhivago divides his feelings and his body between two women. This appears to be fine. The two ladies approve; they fall in love with him and speak no word against him. For me, in the same situation, there would be no mercy: I am the common man.

I buy a newspaper and look for articles about the upcoming fight. The weighing-in: 63.3 and 62.4 kilos. I study the police blotter. Suicides, zero. Attempts, zero. Arsonist arrested. Turns out to be a member of the Marcos Paz Volunteer Fire Brigade. He confesses, explains that he set fire to a number of things in order "to enable the volunteer fire brigade to demonstrate its courage and skill."

A dissatisfied man: There are firemen but no fires.

Governments should be formed exclusively of genuinely dissatisfied people. The kind who won't resign themselves to anything, who will always demand that everything be improved.

There can be fire without firemen; that's how it was for millions of years. But a fireman without a fire to put out must feel that his condition is absurd. If he's a normal man, it must cause him anguish.

He's like me. I, too, am oppressed by what I don't do. But I don't do it.

At the stadium, I don't sit with my colleagues. I'm one among many in the bellowing stands.

I shout and curse. When blood spurts from an eyebrow laid open by an uppercut I yell for the eye to be smashed, and that I'll spit on the corpse of the man who holds back, the man who doesn't fight hard enough. I clamor for violence and destruction.

This is normal: My belligerence is collective and my atrocities mingle in the air with everyone else's.

I give vent. One night a week. On other days, outside the stadium, you can't incite anyone to kill his fellow man or let off steam about everything that offends and diminishes you.

On Sunday I manage to elude Julia; on Monday I cannot elude the boss.

No sooner is he informed of my presence in the editorial offices than he sends his secretary to tell me I shouldn't even think about turning the story in, it's far too late now.

On my desk are two envelopes: One of them, manila, must have Marcela's photos inside. The other has the agency's name printed on it, and also my name, typed. Its contents are unknown. I open it first.

It contains more notes from Bibi. Immediately, from the first piercing words, they act upon me, make me uneasy.

Durkheim says, "In families where repeat suicides occur, they're often performed almost identically. They take place not only at the same age . . ."

They take place . . . at the same age, he says.

"but even in the same way. In one case hanging is preferred, in another asphyxiation or falling from a high place. In one oft-cited case, the resemblance is even greater; the same weapon was used by a whole family at intervals of several years."

My father's pearl-handled gun that Mamá keeps in the dresser.

But Durkheim maintains that this is because of the contagious influence on the minds of surviving family members, and that it has yet to be proven that suicide is an inherited trait; if an individual whose family included mad people and suicides kills himself, it's not because his parents took their own lives but because they were mad. Durkheim says this.

Oppression makes you weak.

If Durkheim says it then it comes as a relief, though in point of fact I don't know who Durkheim is. An authority on the subject, perhaps. The Louis Pasteur, the Marie Curie of suicide. Who knows.

I read: "Durkheim repeats..."

Still Durkheim. I hesitate, given the risk of a further addendum which could reignite my suspicion that suicide might be hereditary. Why does Bibi keep at this? Does she know? Is my soul so transparent?

Durkheim repeats something recounted by Falret.

A young girl of nine learned that an uncle on the father's side had intentionally killed himself. The news affected her greatly: She had heard it said that insanity is hereditary...

Insanity, not suicide.

> ...While she was in this sad state her father voluntarily put an end to his own existence.

Suicide.

> From that time onward she felt herself absolutely destined to a violent death. She had no other thought than the impending end and repeated incessantly: "I must perish like my father and my uncle! Thus is my blood tainted!" She tries to kill herself...

There it is, finally: heredity.

> However, the man she believed to be her father was not actually her father. To free her from her fears her mother confessed the truth and arranged an interview for her with her real father. The great physical resemblance between them caused the patient's doubts to disappear instantly. She at once gave up all thought of suicide; her cheerfulness steadily returned and she regained her health.

Happy ending.

Do I like this? Do I not like it? The question isn't whether this is to my taste or whether life imitates novels. This particular case lays all my doubts out before me, wants to disorient me, torture me, until it restores me to life and health. Should I keep pondering it?

I go to where Bibi sits, translating, and tell her that with this latest note about heredity she's done enough for now, thanks. I'll do some more research locally, to illustrate the piece with figures and a few clinical cases.

She asks whether I have my own theory. I tell her I don't but whatever I come up with will provide a basis to confirm or challenge this. "Challenge Durkheim?" She's astonished, though she quickly acknowledges, "Others have done so." She doesn't specifically say that these others knew more about it than I do, and doesn't notice that she's thus opened another path toward doubt; if Durkheim is not the irrefutable Einstein of suicide then his theory of non-inheritance lacks relativity. But I bear up with equanimity.

I ask after Piel Blanca and she points out that it would not be a good idea for me to call her at her job. She says we can look for her that night in the bowling alley, though she doesn't know whether she'll show up.

Marcela sees the envelope with the photos.

"None of them are of any use?"

"I didn't look at them. I didn't do the story."

She loses interest.

She smokes. "We're bogged down," she says.

I say, "Yes. We are."

I suggest, "This afternoon—"

She cuts me off. "I can't. I'm seeing the father."

I translate. "The old guy."

It's made me a little angry.

I ask her why: Why will she be seeing him.

"Because we agreed to."

"And he's taking you to his house? The wife will be there—"

"He's not taking me, he's inviting me. And not to his house, to the Galley Slave. Any other questions, *patrón*?"

We have two months to do the work. How many cases can we hope to observe during that time?

I turn to the Statistics Department.

The expert lady who's hearing me out murmurs, "Ah, codes 970 to 979." I'm about to say "Exactly" when I realize I have no idea what codes 970 to 979 are. I tell her so and she says, "Those are the suicides. Under the international statistical classification of causes of death. The codes for homicide are 980 to 983."

She adds, "There are a lot more 970 to 979s than 980 to 983s."

Understood. How many 970s (and thereafter) can we expect over the course of a brief period—a week, a month?

She issues her response with professional exactitude. The typical rate for an industrialized Western city can go from two suicides per day for a city of six million to one every six days for a city of half a million.

Nevertheless, she continues, rates are unstable and highly variable, especially in America. They depend on social conditions that vary a great deal from country to country. She can only give me an approximate idea.

At the same time, there are also distinctive patterns of distribution across the seasons. Since people tend to kill themselves more frequently in spring and summer, a city of half a million may have a case every two or three days during certain months, but fewer cases during the colder months.

*

At the bowling alley, Bibi shows me which three fingers to put in the ball, how far toward the lane to step, the proper inclination of the body. It's not enough to enable me to knock over any pins. My projectiles veer here and there and seem irresistibly drawn toward the gutters.

I'd rather Piel Blanca took over for me, but she never shows up.

With Bibi, we order something off the menu and share it for dinner. Before that, she drank gin, neat. "Shall we roll?" she suggests, and takes my hand, which was resting on the table. I say "Yes," then say, "I'd like that." "Who wouldn't?" she comments, which, though I don't know precisely what she means by "roll," leads me to believe my conjecture is correct. I make so bold as to inquire, "Where?"

"Around here," she says airily.

She guides me to the 4L.

She steers with her right hand, hanging her left arm outside the car as if to cool it off or pretend it can fly. She hums.

I wait.

We're driving along side streets, semirural, overgrown with weeds.

She tells a spicy story, laughs at it, and, releasing the steering wheel altogether for a moment, squeezes my knee. I stroke her thigh. She says "No," which is not an impediment. She insists, "No," and stops the car.

"Here?" I query.

"Here what?"

"Quick question," I say. "What does 'roll' mean?"

"Driving around, driving around anywhere."

I don't believe her and try to kiss her. She stops me. I remain expectant. How things go from here depends on her.

She apologizes. "It's not that I don't want to. The thing is, I'm otherwise engaged . . ."

"To be married?"

"I wouldn't say that yet. Maybe sometime soon."

Which is all the same to me. As I said: Every woman has somebody.

We drive back to the center of town, without anger.

That night, Julia has abandoned her aggression. Even better, she accedes to my desires, as docile as ever.

Afterward, in a moment of attention I notice that she gives the impression of being oblivious to what's around her and, at the same time, somewhat frightened. But I don't ask.

On her own, she begins to voice what's gnawing at her. She had a dream.

She saw herself in a hole underground, and an animal was hounding her. She cried out for help, called to her father. The animal shape-shifted into her father, who in reality no longer exists. Julia thought she was saved but the father devoured her.

She asks what I make of this. I tell her I haven't formed an opinion.

She says, "It's so awful," and insists on trying to determine whether it's some dark omen.

I tell her that it isn't, I can still recall some vague notions from Freud: the child's fear of being eaten alive in the cradle, the father's cannibalism as a symbol of authority and power, the totem, I believe, something having to do with incest. But all of it, in any case, seems more rigorously applicable to the male than to the female.

Julia remains the same, as if I hadn't explained anything. I'm aware of this but add, nevertheless, "If I were to have the same dream, it would, with far greater certainty, have this meaning: That I'm afraid my father might devour, castrate, or kill me."

"Your father died," she reminds me.

All the same he can lead me to my death, he can kill me, if he persists in my memory and draws me to him. That's what I think.

Julia remains lost in thought, while I reflect that what I've just said shouldn't be renewed cause for concern because I can also understand it as a conjecture made with regard to something impersonal that doesn't affect me.

Julia is disturbed now and it shows. "There's more," she admits, downcast.

The dream went on. The animal turned back into an animal, a wild boar that charged at her in silence. Julia defended herself by flinging mud at it, the mud they both were wallowing in. The struggle was endless; at every second, Julia could have been torn apart by its tusks. There was no respite, no way out, no possibility the dream could end.

I say it sounds like a corner of hell.

Julia looks at me and puts her arms around me in despair.

She repeats that it's horrible. Worse, she thinks it must be, for her, a condemnation, a punishment.

I ask why. She says the wild boar was me.

I take *The Drowned World* to bed with me—I make it to page 40—and also *The World Below*, which I don't even open.

What will help me erase this day?

It won't be erased. Julia's dream keeps coming back. The boar. Papá: the totem that comes for you, that eats you.

We still dream "the old-fashioned way." Our nightmares are straight out of *The Divine Comedy*. Ugolino.

When the new generations reach the age of suffering and start being persecuted by their dreams, will their nights be filled with medieval witches or sci-fi clones?

I set the books aside, to sleep.

If my father persists, and draws me to him... I look at the calendar on the wall. If only I could dream of an aquarium, please God!

But what I dream is that I'm walking around naked.

Bibi brings me word: Blanca has news. We'll see her tomorrow night.

Julia broke down during class and resigned from her job at the school.

I imagine it must be pregnancy but don't say so. She complains—over the phone—that I don't even ask why she fell apart. I ask. She says it was a reaction, disgust, fear. The principal read the homework. There'll be a review, he initiated the process today.

At the café, Marcela wonders, "And the series?" I promise her that we'll spring into action the day after tomorrow. She gives me an indulgent smile.

When I ask whether the old man tried to seduce her, she doesn't bristle or withdraw. She admits he did, with resignation and a spark of complicity in her eyes.

I'm pleased to have been right and would like to kiss her. She tells me about it.

This man needs to love; he doesn't ask to be loved himself

but wants only understanding and tenderness. He's just suffered a disappointment, a double encounter with death.

He met a young woman, living on her own with a small daughter. He helped her out with money. One day he realized he loved her. Though—he told Marcela—he'd acted out of compassion and generosity, he expected at least some affection in return. They had long talks, again and again, but she would never agree to any intimacy. He threatened to kill himself, showed her a vial of poison. The woman repeated that she loved him, but in a particular way, as a father. They separated, each holding fast to their position.

The man had dinner with his wife and son. He was completely immersed in his thoughts and didn't notice the boy except twice: once when he knocked over a glass and again as he was leaving, because he stood for longer than usual in the doorway, turned toward them. Once he was alone with his wife, he felt pity for her but told himself, I must have love in my life—or nothing.

He locked himself in his study and prayed. He was aware of having committed a sin. He spent a long time in prayer.

He waited until midnight, alert for the telephone.

When all hope was exhausted, distraught and in pain because the young woman was allowing him to die, he sat down at his desk and opened the vial. But he felt guilty about selfishly abandoning his family, and convinced himself that, at the very least, he had to make up a reason other than the real one, and say goodbye to them.

He wrote to his wife and was writing to his son when he fainted.

When he came to, dawn was at the window. He searched for the vial but it had fallen and spilled all of its toxic liquid.

"Which means," I say, "that while the father dozed off

during his blackmailing of the young lady, the son was passing over to the other world without asking permission or giving any warning signs. But only if we choose to overlook the suspicion that the whole thing is a contemptible farce invented out of whole cloth to convince you to feel sorry for him and give him what he would call your 'intimacy.'"

But Marcela thinks he's sincere.

He's not. His son's action suggested to him, after the fact, a new chapter for his own biography. A father and son *cannot* commit suicide on the same date without any prior agreement, without either one knowing what the other is doing. I can't conceive of that, I wouldn't be able to understand it. I am a normal man.

I don't argue. I've warned her about intimacy. Really, if I got worked up, it was only because I'm defending her.

We're in the Citroën, Marcela and I, racing toward a boy who's climbed up to a high place.

We reach an area where all traffic has ground to a halt.

I see him. His arms and legs are wrapped around the iron base of a giant billboard that tops a monolithic eight-story apartment building. He doesn't move, neither letting go nor starting to climb back down.

I question the people around me. They say he's been up there half an hour. What's he waiting for? To be saved, says a man, incredulously.

Maybe not. Maybe he's only postponing the plunge. I think he's just beginning to understand a very important thing: If he jumps, his body will feel the horrible suck of the void for the full twenty-five meters down and will then be crushed against the pavement. He'll die, for sure, but only after that. Certainly, when he was considering this from street level, it didn't strike him the same way.

The firemen's mechanical ladder reaches the eighth floor and one of them climbs up.

Marcela is busy with her work. First she leans out a window with the telephoto lens, then she goes off to stand on a nearby rooftop.

I glimpse a fortuitous pay phone, just inside the door of a pharmacy. I call the agency and ask to speak to the boss. I tell him I can give a blow-by-blow account of the whole thing without losing sight of it. He gives me the okay and starts taping the conversation.

A silence that doesn't exist in this city has fallen, punctured only by the sound of brakes and engines at the edge of the traffic jam. The crowd wants to hear. But the fireman who's reached the top of the ladder is so close to the individual that the two can negotiate without raising their voices.

No doubt he's trying to convince him to get down, and his gestures keep the spectators as riveted as they are ignorant. Until the young man explodes: "Stop looking at me! That's enough!" The fireman seems to calculate that if he pushes any harder the guy will throw himself off the billboard.

The fireman gives up, but the moment he's down the ladder a policeman goes up.

Decisive, courageous, he reaches the top swiftly, takes out a weapon, and aims it at the would-be suicide.

The crowd lets out a universal exclamation.

I realize it's a spray gun, though it looks like the kind that fires bullets. But I can't imagine what the policeman is trying to do.

Then immediately I see it: The boy has started moving, he's slipping back toward the balcony. He was going to kill himself, then thought the policeman was about to shoot him. He felt death approaching and no longer wished to die.

Many of the spectators leave, returning to the day's ordinary hustle and bustle, though quite a few stay, watching to see if anything goes wrong and the teenager falls.

I finish giving my report to the agency.

Like me, another person next to me was passing along a message, though hers went higher: a middle-aged woman, praying.

None of that actually happened. I dreamed the whole thing.

Bibi is hypnotizing me with her card catalogue and now I'm having nightmares.

There's a story, I believe, about someone who threw himself into a river and a customs officer came along with a rifle and in the end the would-be suicide went calmly home.

All customs officers, if they don't have a name, are called Rousseau.

Bibi orders gin. I hint, with some malice, at how that will end.

She assures me, gently teasing, that even if she has a little too much tonight, she won't invite me to go for a roll with her. Piel Blanca asks with a nervous stammer what "go for a roll" means. "You see?" I accuse her. "That expression of yours gives rise to misunderstandings." "I thought it meant something good," Blanca says defensively. "I just wanted an explanation." "But it's something bad," I tell her. "It produces no results." Piel Blanca plunges into the wordlessness of a person who is cautious or shy.

In general, I like her quite a bit. I long to touch her.

After the waiter has served us the first drink and is distracted by other tables, the photos reappear, in her hands.

There's a slip of paper clipped to each one. I pick up the first. A name—Adriana Pizarro—a date, a home address, a little map. The map shows the position of the body, where it fell: furniture, doors and window, bloodstains, weapon. I exchange it with Bibi for the other photo of a suicide with wide-open eyes, which bears a different name—Juan Tiflis —date, home address, and map.

Piel Blanca gives us a moment to look them over. Then she speaks.

Adriana Pizarro was a forty-six-year-old spinster, a school-teacher, with a savings account and small investments. At forty-two, she took a trip to Europe. When she returned, she said she'd have to go back. She hinted at a relationship. But never—according to her family—did she receive a letter, not from Spain, France, or Italy, as if she hadn't met anyone. Only tourist brochures and leaflets with updated rates for hotels. Some of her relatives claimed she experienced hallucinations. "She saw things," one testified, "and may have killed herself during a crisis."

Piel Blanca points to the gun in the photo and notes that it's unusual for her to have chosen that method; women generally prefer gas, cyanide, or sleeping pills, while a few of them hang themselves. "She used a small one, .22 caliber, as if she didn't want to do too much damage to herself. And she succeeded—she aimed right where she needed to."

Juan Tiflis was a man of some wealth, altruistically inclined and spiritual; he was a dealer in documents, a financer of automobile raffles, an art collector and seller of works that grew in value, a patron of the philharmonic and the orphans' home. He was a person of elegant manners and, in his own way, an idealist, according to the friends and acquaintances called on to provide testimony. He left behind a single written line, very much in keeping with his image: "I move forward into the calm darkness."

This guidance is helpful; now I know where to go, what to focus on. Yet not one of Blanca's references casts any light on the reason for the terrified stare and the somber grimace of pleasure. "No doctor or psychiatrist noticed those details? The file doesn't contain any mention of them, cast any light?" No, it does not. "People from Forensics were involved. Wasn't that facial expression out of the ordinary, quite different from what they normally see?" Yes, it stood out. "Did they remember it?" No, they didn't notice it at first; they only started thinking about it after they studied the photos.

I don't feel indebted to her, but I figure Blanca is expecting some acknowledgment. I invite her and Bibi to dinner. We leave, then have to wait for Blanca, who's taking her time adjusting some undergarment. I consult Bibi on what I can do for her, for Blanca. She says Blanca likes to dance. I don't, but I can.

We have dinner and I'm obliged to dance with both of them. It's not much fun. But Piel Blanca doesn't reject close contact. I invite her out another night. Thursday? Thursday it is. Just the two of us, that goes without saying.

We go our separate ways.

I leave Julia out of it.

I wander away from the busier streets. The heat has broken. I'm clearheaded, fine.

There's plenty of night ahead. I could go looking for a

woman. Or walk to where Adriana Pizarro did it. It's not time to go home yet; all I'd see there would be dark outlines, the sleeping household. The investigation will begin tomorrow. Tomorrow! How many tomorrows do I have left?

Tomorrow I could change my life. But I can't change my profession. I am my profession. If I don't change my profession, I can't change my life.

Change Julia for someone else. But exchanging one woman for another changes nothing.

Change my memories. The past can't be changed, it governs us, usually. Thirty-three years ago I was granted this body to which has since been added habits, ideas, a certain way of eating. At seventeen, I had it all wrong. I come from before.

I have a yesterday, I don't know if I'll have a tomorrow. I'm certain of just one thing: that at some moment I will die.

I dream about the woman who's my English professor.

She tells me to study, that I have to get out of there.

She seems to be telling me to escape.

Interlude with Animals

BIBI GETS me started with the section about animals:

> Suicide of a horse. The trainers try to make him cover
> a mare. He refuses. In the end they succeed in making
> him do it. The horse, who knows he was born from that
> mare, intentionally flings himself off a cliff. (Aristotle.)

"See that picture? It's done in tempera. What does it show?"

"The sea. Within the curve of a deserted sandy beach. In the background, a tree."

"And under the tree, what do you see?"

"A couple, sitting in the shade."

"No, only two faint strips of color. Look closer. If I hadn't pointed them out, you wouldn't have noticed. The painting has always been like that, ever since it was made. Adriana took a long time to discover all its details, only after she saw the sea for the first time on her trip. Then she showed me 'the couple,' who were nothing new to me. She said, 'Those who are in love must seek refuge somewhere.' Then she started worrying because she was seeing bathers setting up beach umbrellas. Later, she was upset because, she said, tourists had discovered the beach. When her imagination had entirely filled the tempera painting with people, she started populating that oil painting over there, the one of a forest. During the day, she found woodcutters in it, at night, lost children."

"Was she ever examined by a psychiatrist?"

"In all other respects she was completely normal."

María Pizarro, the widow of Señor Candé, is Adriana Pizarro's sister. She's putting up some resistance to reliving all that happened with Adriana.

She won't allow photographs, not even of the bedroom. We ask her for a picture of Adriana. She'll allow us to see one but not reproduce it.

Did she see her dead? She's the one who found her. The eyes, the mouth? "As if she hadn't died."

The daughter, who's about seventeen, walks us back to the Citroën. The intransigent mother stands in the front hallway, the door ajar.

Speaking in a low voice, the girl says she'll bring us a picture of her aunt and the photos from Europe.

The house that belonged to Juan Tiflis is no longer there, nor can the neighbors provide his wife's current address. Only one fact can they agree upon unanimously: Despite everything, he left her penniless.

From the foundation the house once rested on now rises a structure of iron and cement. The construction company gives me the number of this future hotel's owner, and he gives me the name of the notary who witnessed the deed of sale, and the notary gives me the address of Tiflis's widow, which turns out to be the address of the house that's been demolished. (Four trips, back and forth.)

At the philharmonic they were barely acquainted with Tiflis's wife; she no longer visits the orphans' home, nor does her name appear in the phone book, and the local electoral rolls are years out of date. (Four plus three: seven trips.)

Tiflis's wife isn't a suicide, I hope. At Missing Persons, I ask the police if they have any information about her. (Eight trips.)

Señorita Candé on the phone. She can't make it, she'll do it another day, as soon as she can. Meanwhile, here's a number to call: Tío Eduardo. Tío Eduardo is "special."

Tío Eduardo, a polished individual, poses for Marcela.

He states that he has no fear of public opinion and even less of his sister's opinion.

He divulges information rapidly. "My late sister, Adriana, was afraid of herself when she was alive."

" . . . "

"She suffered from a terror of not being one individual, of multiplying herself: She was everyone else. If she had an argument with someone, she was also that other person. If she went to the theater, the actors and the spectators were all her, multiplied many times over. She considered these other beings into whom she projected herself to be her enemies. Sometimes she would disappear: She couldn't find herself, not in the mirror, not in her bed, not in her own clothes. Then her fear functioned in reverse: She was neither one person nor many, she was less than one, she'd erased herself."

I comment that his version of the story is quite different from the one his sister María gave us.

"Who put you in touch with me?" he asks, deliberately.

"Her daughter."

"You see?" And he smiles, inviting me to understand.

I'm ready to ask him about the corpse's facial expression

but can't because for no reason I can fathom he cuts me off. "I beg you, let's drop this for tonight." He adds, "My home is open to you," then bids us farewell.

I'm convinced that if she puts on her Card Catalogue persona for me again, Bibi will save me from innumerable research rooms, interviews, inquiries, postponements, incomprehensions, inanities. Doctor, I need information about your specialty; doctor, would you please give me your opinion? Doctor, how much is known about this condition? What do you anticipate? Where might I confirm that? I've been there before and would rather not: Egotism is rampant among rival colleagues. "You'll see right through him," a doctor once said to me about another doctor.

I thank Bibi but ask her to please cut it out with the section on horses. I'm experiencing no difficulties with quadruped suicides at the moment, and I am actually dealing with a crazy-woman suicide which also happens to be the case the boss asked me to investigate.

I tell her that Piel Blanca's facts have driven me into a thicket. I tell her about the contradictory and incomplete versions offered by the brother and the sister.

She listens, brimming with interest, or so it appears, then speaks. "Ah, yes, a crazy woman who committed suicide. Because they have to believe that people kill themselves because they're alone, because they're sick, because they're old, because they're too poor, because they're too rich, because other people mocked their standards or their ambitions, because their papá and mamá used to quarrel over their little heads, or for love (very few), or for want of love, or out of shame, pride, imitation, mysticism, freedom, ideas, and other noble things. But mainly because they're crazy."

"Yes," I say.

"But it's not all madness. Some women kill themselves because they're pregnant, even when their own husbands are the fathers. They're terrified of the prospect of suffering."

I ask whether she's pregnant and she cuts off that angle with a curt "No." She goes on.

"Suicide increases with alcohol use, which makes people bolder, also with heat and urban living, with depression brought on by the arrival of autumn, with industrialization and social isolation. It also spikes, proportionally, among the more educated and wealthier classes; doctors are now more likely to commit suicide, but in earlier periods—the nineteenth century—it was members of the military.

"Statistics," she says. She opens a notebook. "Italy: for every civilian suicide, five military suicides; United States, eight and a half; Austria, ten."

"Austria, Vienna: the waltzes," I say.

"Professionals take their own lives more often than people in business or manual laborers do, but manual laborers do so more frequently than skilled laborers. Among young people, students are most likely to do it."

I hazard a supposition that suicides are more frequently male than female. Bibi confirms this, but adds that women attempt suicide in greater numbers, and that more recently, in certain countries, women have been committing suicide as often as men, possibly because of their growing incorporation into general activities.

"Moreover," she explains, "old people commit suicide more often than the young do, but the young attempt suicide and fail more often than the old."

"Are there more suicides among married people like you?"

She consults the notebook. "No, there are more suicides among single people like me."

She goes on. "In the West, whites commit suicide more often than Blacks. In the East, they throw themselves into the Ganges, or off a cliff, or into the mouth of a volcano, or they set themselves on fire or have themselves buried alive to appease their gods. In Africa, suicide is a way to flee from family disputes, castration, impotence, and leprosy."

"Now let's bring it home."

"All right. In South America, it's the same as among primitive peoples: Here, too, family disputes are the number one reason. Nevertheless, prior to the Space Age, Latin Americans had the highest rate of romantic suicides. 'They don't understand us' (standoff between Montagues and Capulets), 'She's marrying someone else,' 'He changed.'"

"Though the men," I reflect, "can easily remedy that by getting laid a few times or having some drinks."

"Yes," Bibi replies, "but they kill her, then kill themselves, and if they take to red wine instead, they start seeing flying rats: alcoholism, mental illness, suicide. And with that we come full circle: Those most likely to commit suicide are—"

"Right, I know: crazy people."

"Yes, crazy people, which is an extremely vulgar and entirely incorrect thing to call them. In serious terms, the mentally ill fall into distinct categories: neurotics, psychotics, and abnormal personalities. Usually the ones who sentence themselves to suicide are suffering from melancholy, the sickness of depression. Not only do they destroy themselves, they're propagandists; they're the type that also kills children 'so they won't suffer.' What can be done about it? Psychiatrists for all!"

Bibi adds, "But, I don't have any specifics on any of this."

She says she'll work on it, it's only a matter of time; she wants me to introduce her to Tío Eduardo. And she has no intention of cutting it out with the animals, no matter what I say.

I wait for Blanca where we'd agreed.

When she shows up, I see she's made an effort, the hair salon and all the rest of it. She's "all dressed up"—or, in other words, quite scantily clad.

My suit and shirt have been on since this morning, which must be apparent; Piel Blanca shoots me a disapproving glance. But her outfit won't be as noticeable in the place we're headed for, the Momotombo.

At the Momotombo they seat us in a corner on a piece of upholstered furniture that we share with other couples whose faces we'd be unable to tell apart.

We hold back while the drinks are arriving. Then we step onto the small dance floor and spend a long time there. We confine our movement to a tiny space, which isn't exactly dancing, and each time the music stops we stay put until it starts again so as not to lose possession of our sixty square centimeters. She's in my arms all the while, naturally.

I've kissed her two or three times and by now she accepts my hands but doesn't participate.

Impossible to talk; with all the noise, it would take an enormous effort to be heard.

She indicates that her feet hurt and I make a gesture to suggest she take off her shoes. But it's impossible to dance with the shoes in one hand while also holding each other, and if she leaves the shoes somewhere we might not find them later.

So we go back to the banquette where the ice in our whiskeys has melted.

Conversation is impossible here, too, but it's slightly easier to make yourself understood.

In any case, I'd prefer for our bodies to make themselves understood.

Piel Blanca is generous toward my intentions, though passive. At a certain point in the proceedings she imposes restrictions that undo my optimism about a rapid consummation.

As I'm trying to make up for lost ground by growing more demanding, Piel Blanca asks if I would marry her.

I pretend not to have heard what she said, and ask what she's asking me: Is it whether I would marry her afterward?

And she says, "No, before."

I tell her I have nothing against her but in general I don't marry anyone.

She wants to know why and I realize I'm not prepared to answer that question. I tell her I don't marry anyone "on principle," but I can still love her all the same.

This does not produce results.

I'll have to get back together with Julia.

The young Candé girl brings us the photographs. Seeing her alone, without her family around, I'm impressed by her melancholy, like Venice in wintertime. Marcela shuffles through the stack of pictures. I thought she'd made her selection, but she's still looking for a vacation snapshot of Adriana with Signore X.

The niece would like to know what we know. There's no reason not to play fair: I hand her the one photo she doesn't have and may not have seen before, the one of her aunt, dead.

She takes a long look, absorbed. I might almost imagine

she's discovered what intrigues us about it. Of all the people this case has brought me into contact with, she's the one with the most alert mind. (Piel Blanca is a bit of a bore.)

She hands the photo back to me, without comment. Even so, she offers us another lead: Tía Alejandra.

Card Catalogue:

> Another aspect, who does it the most: It's not the Swedes (bad reputation) but the Germans from the two Germanys (statistic of the World Health Organization). After the two Germanys are Hungary, Austria, Czechoslovakia, Finland, and Japan. Highest national rate: East Germany, average of 28 suicides per 100,000 inhabitants. Lowest: Egypt, 0.1 for 1959. Sweden's rate of 17 is lower than that of 8 other European nations, despite its fame as the magic kingdom of people who don't want to stick around any longer. Did the Swedes seek this reputation? No, it came from outside, only one factor among many in a subtle and skilled disparagement campaign against their nation.

I tell Marcela, "We can bring Bibi along. She likes this story and she's useful." Marcela wonders whether I have some particular interest in Bibi.

I say I do but it's not producing results; she has someone else and finds me unpleasant. "It must be the last guy. She doesn't have anyone now," she says. "Every woman does," I reply. Marcela doesn't say that she doesn't but then I haven't asked her.

Bibi would prefer we go see Tío Eduardo again, but I point

out that Tía Alejandra might offer us a third version. We climb into the 4L, drive to the house, and the maid tells us she went to town and there's no one home, as if she herself, the maid, weren't someone. But really, what can she do for us.

I suggest to Marcela that we head for the cemetery, which is within walking distance, and I let Bibi, who's stayed in the car, know we're heading over there. She wants to know what for. I say for whatever you want: another item on the agenda.

She follows us. At the cemetery office, while a chubby woman scans the register to find "Juan Tiflis," Bibi does what I should have done and asks a second employee whether suicides are buried in a separate area.

This young woman, who's quite timid and doesn't know much, makes no reply but checks with her more decisive colleague, or boss, who responds with a question—"Whether we do what, señora?"—then disdainfully answers that no, please, where would you get an idea like that from. This is a serious provocation for Bibi who, at no one's request, lets her know "where from": from the church, for which suicide is an insult to God and the worst of all sins because it leaves no opportunity for repentance. After fifteen centuries of this, how can they remain unaware, as apparently they are, of the distinction that the church makes with respect to suicides? And not Catholics alone: Before and after the revolutionary events of the early 1800s, suicides have been separated from other corpses. For the suicide, nothing but burial at the crossroads. In France, the corpse is put on trial, and all over the world, the body is dragged facedown through the street, or hung, or burned, or has a stake pounded through its face.

Got that? Well then, where's Juan Tiflis?

He had not endured the slightest discrimination. The heavyset woman gives us his coordinates, such and such a pavilion, such and such a level, niche number...as if she were revealing a sacrilege she did not commit but by which she might find herself imperiled, unaware that this is a cemetery run by the city government and belonging to the state, which renders Bibi's question about whether certain religious precepts hold any weight here irrelevant. I think I could have asked it myself. I also think it was a trick question.

As we walk toward the pavilion, Marcela raises an objection to Bibi. "Why fifteen centuries and not the twenty centuries of the Christian era?"

"Because the formal condemnation of suicide doesn't happen until AD 500 or 600, when the church is organized. You must know that," Bibi scolds. Marcela, at times so naive, grows visibly upset.

I let out a sarcastic chortle, aimed at both of them.

"We're in a cemetery," Bibi admonishes.

The niche is situated in a rather modest section. Marcela uses her camera flash to light it up.

Who takes care of things around here? A man with a feather duster, bucket, and ladder. He asks which grave and whether we brought flowers. I tell him to go on cleaning and chat him up about the widow. He sees her here quite a bit, though not at regular intervals.

He affirms that this is the most prayed-over grave, "because souls that depart without being called must be saved." He adds, "Poor man, he must have had his reasons"—in case we're relatives of the deceased or maybe in hope of a tip. Since the tip, when it comes, is larger than he could have hoped for, he understands he'll need to do a little more, and what he needs to do is very simple and honest: Ask the widow for her address and pass the information along to me at the agency.

Missing Persons has yet to locate Señora Tiflis. I ring up Blanca and she points out that when I call her at work, I jeopardize her situation.

Yes, and that's exactly what I did to Julia, too. I jeopardized her situation.

Bibi ends up missing out on Tía Alejandra; an Italian correspondent is keeping her busy.

Tía Alejandra confirms both of her siblings' statements: For Adriana, the paintings in the living room were like television screens with a fixed decor to which she added and removed actors; for Adriana, her own face could, at times, be the face of all humankind; at other times "that which can be seen" was lost to her, along with her whole body. But the other siblings, María and Eduardo, had neglected to tell me something else about Adriana. "If she took her own life, it wasn't because she was, in certain ways, so odd. She did it because of the voices."

"What voices?"

"The voices that called out to her."

"She heard voices? Could anyone else hear them? Could you?"

"No, señor. Only Adriana. They spoke to her."

"Do you believe that?"

"Of course not."

"Sorry, I don't quite know how to ask this ... No one ever managed to persuade her to seek treatment?"

"Treatment for what?"

"Well, whatever a specialist might diagnose."

"But Adriana wasn't sick!"

"The hell she wasn't. What about all the symptoms?"

"They weren't real, she was making them up!"

The señora remonstrates against my incomprehension.

I turn to Marcela, who doesn't help but is keeping busy: With Tía Alejandra, at last, she can do as she pleases, without asking permission, without any posing, without her realizing what's happening.

Coffee reconciles us and when I deem the señora sufficiently disarmed I ask about the face.

Yes, she'd had a long look at Adriana's dead body, in order to hold on to her image. I encourage her to be more specific. "What was her expression?" she muses. "Very, very sweet. It was the face of someone who's sleeping, having pleasant dreams."

I show her the photo. She considers it without growing emotional, then places it back in my hands. "It's pure cruelty," she states. "Things like that should not be preserved." And she kindly offers me another cup of coffee.

Tío Eduardo grows animated and expansive, because Bibi is more stimulating than Marcela, I think.

He wants his image to be seen. He asks when the photos of him will be published and, disregarding my attempt at a vague answer, lets us know that the newspapers have already featured him and that, in fact, he enjoys a certain notoriety. He shows us proof, clippings from old publications. "Winner,

Regional Chess Tournament." "An Honest Citizen" (returns lost money). A photo of him and another man with a fish (a thirty-kilo black drum, caught in the river).

Bibi is knowledgeable about fishing, even about fishing in inland waters, and I let them fraternize for a while until I decide he's ready and break in with my questions.

I want to find out whether he knew that Adriana heard voices. He says he did but learned it secondhand, through his other sisters. Why?

"Modesty," he confesses, and that's also why he'd prefer I didn't keep asking questions.

But Bibi is interested and, with considerable self-assurance, intervenes. "Did the voices make indecent propositions?"

Bibi cannot be denied, though he's blushing. "No," he says, "not exactly."

Bibi: "Then what?"

He hesitates. "I can only say this to you ..." Then he says it so everyone can hear. "Not exactly indecent propositions, no, but something close to that: The voices only came when she was in her underwear."

Bibi: "And she ... she liked it?"

"She may have," he admits, embarrassed.

"What did the voices say?" I ask.

"That they were waiting for her, that she had to join them."

"Would you say these were the voices of spirits, or quite the contrary?"

"They were the voices of spirits because they were urging her to abandon the material world."

Bibi: "They were urging her. You agree, yes? So, there *were* voices. Right?"

Tío Eduardo may be feeling cornered. He argues. "Adriana was ill."

I say, "But without medical care. She needed a psychiatrist."

"You think so? Adriana wasn't that type of patient."

Me: "Forgive me, but that's a rather surprising thing for you to say."

"Her illness was physical. She suffered from irregular functioning of some of her organs."

Bibi: "Which organs? The lady parts?"

"Yes. She might have been able to cure herself. She was very attentive to them. She would say she could rebuild them."

"But is there any way?" Bibi inquires, confounded.

"Oh, by mental concentration, you can imagine."

"In short, Señor Pizarro," I rise to my feet and say, "our incredulity, which we cannot hide, pains you. Am I correct?"

"Ah! But this is a huge misunderstanding!" Tío Eduardo has grown radiant, as if suddenly liberated. "You don't believe it? Well, I don't believe it either!"

I feel mocked but also sense that we're dealing with an unfortunate man who is incapable of seeing things clearly. Marcela remains silent and indifferent. Bibi is still curious and wants to verify what she's heard. "You don't believe she heard voices, you don't believe she could really rebuild her own organs?"

Tío Eduardo calmly shakes his head.

Bibi is also calm and scolds him for the deception.

"I didn't deceive you! I wanted to be useful. I thought you believed what Alejandra told you about the voices and I didn't want to make you have to toss out all the work you've been doing for the newspapers. I added the rest on my own. I thought it would make the story more interesting to you."

No, I didn't tell him that Alejandra also thought Adriana was making up the voices.

We've left Tío Eduardo talking to himself. I hear him say, "Anyway, that's my method."

He reclaims Bibi's attention.

"My method," Pizarro confesses, "is always to say the opposite of what I think. That way I get along with everybody."

If I were to accept this last statement, I'd be forced to deduce that since he told us he didn't believe in the voices, he must actually believe in the voices.

I'm about to give up, but I remember the face. Maybe that's a good way to make him focus and listen to me. I ask him about it.

Tío Eduardo switches off his sparkle, lowers his gaze, keeps us waiting for a while, then says, "It was diabolical," which seems to indicate that unlike any of the others he noticed something strange. He describes it. "The mouth was twisted in fear and revulsion but as if to make up for it the eyes seemed to be delighting in the contemplation of some sublime spectacle."

O most refined liar. The niece, who saw the photo, told him about it and he wants to show off his powers of observation. But he's misremembered and got it backward: In the photo the terror is in the eyes, the pleasure in the grimacing mouth.

Bibi later surmises, based on what she knows about Adriana, what she's heard about Eduardo, and what I told her about Alejandra and María de Candé, that these four beings are among the undecided, those who can't make up their minds between reality and unreality. Their proximity to the supernatural doesn't necessarily make them any happier, perhaps the contrary, since their terrors become innumerable.

Marcela: "Do they or don't they believe in things that aren't real?"

Bibi: "They believe, not in all of them, but in three or four that they've fixated on. They think they have some of them under control, while others control them."

I follow their dialogue. I'm not in a position to judge whether Bibi's confident statements are well-grounded in a knowledge of the universe that she may have picked up here and there, or invented by her quick and insightful mind, always able to seize on an apparently convincing explanation.

Whatever the case, she makes thoughts fly upward in me like sparks. Death itself, from one point of view, could be an unreality. For my dead body, death isn't real. For others, for those who are alive, my death is a reality, my dead body the residue of my death. They can prove it: Even if they pound a stake through my face, my dead body won't react.

Ideas flash past like seeds of fire in the night and I don't retain them for the analysis and further reflection that could tell me whether they're coherent with my stance.

Now Bibi wonders whether Alejandra and Eduardo and María de Candé may be tempted to imitate Adriana, may at any moment hear her voice calling out to them.

I think over this prediction and ask myself: And the niece, might she follow them?

I stop.

I pay up and bid them good night. They don't seem to care.

I leave for the supernatural world of the movies.

Since I don't know what to say when I'm with Julia again, I say "*Hola*," and she responds in kind.

After that we're silent, while I expect a reproach and she, I suppose, an explanation.

Maybe I'm supposing wrong because seeing me take no initiative, she speaks, and what she asks is whether I've been ill. Though this comes as a surprise, I tell her yes, I have been. Am I all right now? Perfectly. What was it this time? Same as always. You should see a doctor, she says. I acknowledge that.

(Same as always is the disease I don't have.)

She doesn't look upset or tortured and is so focused on me, seeming to forget herself entirely, that I deduce she isn't holding my absence for the past several days against me, nor have her issues at school grown any worse. Which leads me to conclude it's safe to ask about them.

"And your difficulties?"

She grows serious and says, "Let's not talk about that."

I suspect I was mistaken and something is still going on in the background. I go along with her suggestion because I truly don't want any problems.

I get close to her, which I hadn't done until then, and take her face in my hands. She lets me, eyes full of questions. I give her a very light kiss and she asks if I still love her. I answer "Yes" because I know she'll like that. This instantly becomes the basis for an accusation. "We women like to hear that without having to ask."

I fall silent, guessing her weak protest doesn't mean she's not gratified by my response. In any case I have no doubt I've spoken the truth; I feel good with her and that must mean I love her.

We spend two very pleasurable hours together, and as I'm about to go, she lets me know, in a low and rather pained voice, "Five of the mothers have demanded my resignation."

After a brief delay I react. "That's quite a blow."

She says yes, it is, and I ask whether the principal is fair-minded. She believes he is, but the review, necessarily, must continue until the inspector files his report, and the mothers' petition must be part of the record, it can't be omitted. I tell her that's true and offer to make a declaration myself, to attest, as part of the review, that I requested her collaboration for journalistic purposes, which, I think, fits with an interpretation of what she did as a service to the public. She smiles indulgently and ponders, "And my responsibility?"

I don't insist; she's a responsible little woman, she believes that she's failed in her duty and won't exhaust every resource to keep herself from being punished. Since that's how it is, I find her reaction reasonable.

Arriving home, I run into my brother on the sidewalk while he's putting the car away. I help him close the garage door.

He's just come from receiving his regular injection of sociability: dinner with his buddies the first Friday of every month.

First Friday. Something floods over me and makes me weak: I think of Papá's ending. But only briefly. It passes.

Mauricio, freshly injected, pulls beer out of the refrigerator, keeps me with him, embraces me, full of contentment. He tells me the one about the deaf guys, the one about the blind guys, the one about the crotches, the one about the guy from Andalusia, the one about the vagrant from Chile.

He's making a bit of a racket and a light switches on in his bedroom. Mauricio stammers. The light goes off. He smiles good-naturedly and tells me, "I always behave myself. Did you know that? Always."

I point out that he doesn't need to justify himself. After all, nothing's wrong.

An envelope launches my workday. Bibi has turned back into Card Catalogue and is keeping me supplied.

Under siege by Brutus, the population of Xanthos, in their furor, fed the fire that raged through the city with all manner of combustibles and threw their small children into the flames; men and women flung themselves from the top of walls or killed each other. "Nothing can be done to evade death which they did not do to avoid life." (Montaigne, *Essays*.)

When the Cimbri were defeated at Vercellae, they were met on their retreat by their own wives, who hurled spears at their chests and heads. Those who hadn't fled ran themselves through with their own weapons or submitted to being trampled by oxen. The vengeful women crushed their own children with wagons and hung themselves. (In the year 100, before Christ.)

The Roman authorities deported young Jewish women, sending them off to a life of shame in Rome. The women committed suicide by throwing themselves into the sea. (*Gittin.*)

Jews who were persecuted during the Middle Ages gathered together, killed their children, then took their own lives.

1772: the dilapidated wing of a hospital in France. There's a hook. One after another, fifteen invalids hang themselves from it.

Instances of mass suicide among animals, as well:

> More than a hundred whales committed suicide by
> hurling themselves one after the other onto the beach
> last Thursday, on the island of Cuyo at the center of
> the Philippine archipelago. The Philippine Press Agency
> made the announcement and added that some of the
> cetaceans were up to six meters in length. The inhabit-
> ants of the island testified that a similar phenomenon
> occurred forty years earlier: a large number of whales
> beached themselves, to die together in precisely the
> same spot. (Agence France-Presse, December 10, 1966.)

Bibi answers the phone and beckons me over, "From the
cemetery." For a forgetful instant, I find this strange. "From
the cemetery? Who?"

"The voices, they're calling out to you," Bibi says, mock-
ing me.

He's managed to procure the address, the caretaker of the
niches. The señora didn't want to give it to him, she's afraid
it might be the same ones. Who are "the same ones"? The
ones from the exhumation. When they exhumed the señor's
corpse. What señor? Señor Tiflis. Why did they exhume
him? The gang, the Law...

His facts flap their wings and fly away. "We'll talk more
about this right away," I tell him, then pick up Marcela from
the darkroom and we're off. Bibi is already downstairs in the
4L with the motor running, but the Italian shows up and
she has to stay behind.

According to the caretaker, it was "a gang of individuals"
and charges of "corpse desecration" were later filed. (He
helped take the coffin down and helped pry its lid off, after

it was violated.) The rest was done by the doctor, the judge, and the widow who had to say that yes, this was Señor Tiflis, despite the state that the body was in and the fact that the right hand was missing. The "individuals in the gang," each with a police officer next to him, denied everything: They hadn't cut it off.

I ask when. This winter. My professional memory tells me that I saw no published mention of it. Marcela? No—it's news to her. I comment that this is because of the lack of collaboration. Marcela appears to agree but doesn't express it. I look at her and feel that I love people who are sad and silent.

Tiflis's widow has a niche of her own: She lives in a one-room apartment. Inside are a painting and a dog. The collector's widow possesses only one painting.

She was beautiful. Anyone can see that, looking at her now.

She tells us, overwhelmed, that the case is closed and she can't repeat the accusations because without additional evidence no one will listen to her, and on top of that she's afraid of losing everything. If it's so important to us, then the file can be exhumed as the corpse was. We ask her for it. But she assures us that we won't be able to clear anything up; this is a secret organization full of dangerous individuals.

The window behind her begins to shake: The big dog has jumped up on it, standing on its hind legs, front paws against the glass.

"Don't be afraid, señorita," the widow calms Marcela down. Marcela, whom I've never seen in the grip of intense emotion before, begs pardon. "It was so sudden."

This episode seems to give them a sudden, reciprocal bond,

which the señora affirms by saying, "If you want to be my friend and visit me, you'll have to get used to that. There are days when King does it all the time. When the pigeons fly away, he wants to hunt them. It's his only distraction, he waits for them to go past the window. He's already broken one of the panes and cut his paw on it. I had a double pane put in and can't open the window now because King would throw himself out."

She fills some tiny cups with a friendly liqueur, but her pet has thrown everything out of kilter. We're jammed in there with the dog, the furniture, and no fresh air, and the animal is disturbing us with its relentless stalking of the pigeons. From time to time, it whines impatiently.

Marcela can hardly breathe so the widow sets her selfishness aside, gets to her feet, and orders, "King, come." King does not react. She grabs him by the collar, drags him to the bathroom, and shuts him in.

Saying nothing, Marcela has risen to her feet and taken over the dog's spot next to the window. This complicates the situation because the señora can see that the sacrifice, punishment, or whatever it is she's done to her beloved mastiff, has been to no avail. But Marcela has the right to do as she wishes, of course. I see her so disconnected, languid, and gentle, so abandoned to herself. I feel I could love her.

The señora denies that it might have been a gang. That's not the right term for them—though who knows. Secret society fits them better: a secret society of mystical beings who have no dislike of money and know very well how to get their hands on it. They're quite sinister, though she shouldn't say so, given that her husband was one of them. But he was head and shoulders above the rest of them. She can do no more than what she's already done, and she worries that if she doesn't cease and desist they'll exact some vengeance. I may be able to see the case file and find some leads there, and if I do turn up something that truly compromises them I'll have her gratitude, because in the end, and though it reflects badly on her to say so, she wants revenge, too.

At first she interested me; now she's wearing me out. If she keeps talking I'll have to tell her so, because my head is hurting. Her secret society must be another piece of delirium, like the fantasies peddled by Adriana and her siblings, though the dead man was in fact missing a hand, the caretaker says so. Even if that's true, this investigation is too difficult for me and I don't think that the boss is going to want me to follow up on it and if he does he can go find a younger journalist, someone eager to make a name for himself.

Perhaps as a defense, I distract myself. The nude, a seated woman seen from behind, is in the shape of a pear: From the narrow nape of the neck the body swells toward the fullness of the buttocks. The profile is the widow's face. A different era, but it's her.

I feel the need to get out of there, to be with Marcela.

I take Marcela's hand and she interprets this as a signal for her to say goodbye and thanks me without words.

Even so, when we're back in her Citroën and she turns the key in the ignition and asks what we're doing I say that I don't know what she's doing, but I'm going to the movies.

That night, seated among many others, I hurl insults at the ring. Some swishy fellow (where is he? can anyone see him?) taunts the crowd, but he's got a retinue, whose response to "Hey pipe down! Don't be—" is to throw things at us, anything, Coke bottles, construction debris. Which, obviously, we are not prepared to tolerate. I'm on the receiving end of four punches—the one that stuns me most is to the ear—and I deliver a few myself. After things are straightened out and everyone's calmed down and back in his own seat, I can barely follow the ups and downs of the undercard match. Even so, I understand I have no reason to feel remorse; it wasn't anything personal and I should be happy about the blows I gave in return.

Sunday I again spend a pleasurable moment with Julia. And I remember Marcela.

But with Marcela, I imagine, I'd have to start everything from the very beginning. I mean, the pursuit, some sort of pretext, some sort of formality, some sort of courtship, all the inconvenience.

By Monday the pain where the punch landed is gone. Bibi is with her Italian and not helping; Señorita Candé has let me know she's coming in; the boss is asking about the series; and without Marcela, who hasn't shown up yet, I go see the widow to ask for the file number and the names of the tribunal and her lawyer.

The lawyer says the whole thing is Señora Tiflis's obsessive fantasy and the only reality is the fact that a hand was cut from the dead man's body, which he attributes to graverobbers who steal rings from corpses.

I point out that to steal a ring you only need to sever a finger, and he acknowledges that and concedes that the story may serve some purpose for "a certain kind" of journalism. I say I don't practice "a certain kind" of journalism and he replies, "Forgive me, I didn't mean you. I don't know you." We agree on that.

I explain that my methodology is objective and that I intend to use the case file as my point of departure, if he can arrange for me to see it.

He says he'll cooperate with serious journalism with great pleasure, though certainly not as a favor to the widow, who, sincerely, deserves no such thing, twenty years younger than Tiflis but with quite a history all her own. "You saw the painting? The monumental nude. It's her, she was the model. As you know, señor, he was an art collector. No doubt he found her at loose ends in some artist's studio and she allowed herself to be bought, like a painting. Señor, I believe that Tiflis always secretly despised her, there's no evidence that he allowed her to participate at all in his life, nor, when he shot himself, did he leave her anything material, a letter, or a child, only the dog—you saw it?—a chained maniac of a dog, exactly like the woman who owns it. Animals take after their masters, that is axiomatic."

He says he'll read over the judicial proceedings, as I've asked, he promises me that, but on my end I'll have to dig into other things if I'm truly intent on this, and he'll help me, though he's skeptical. Because with Tiflis, just when you least expect it, you've entered another jurisdiction, the matter of the brotherhood and the rites of death will be revealed at the right moment, that will be for next time; first I have to see the case file; he'll let me know when. I can go now, with confidence.

At the front desk Marcela left a note, not specifically for me: "Back at 4:00." The boss is circling the hallways but doesn't ask about the series or take any notice of me. On my desk is an envelope with a message scrawled by hand: "Greetings,

Blanquita." But nothing inside is from Piel Blanca, only more notes from Bibi.

The dog throws itself down on its master's tomb and lets itself die.

The scorpion pricks itself with its own toxin and perishes.

The drone gives up its life for the privilege of fecundating the queen bee.

While the female and male spiders of a given species mate, the former eats the latter, and the latter does not cease copulating until he dies.

During the migration of a certain type of fish, upstream against the current, those that can't manage to leap up the natural stone steps beat themselves against the rocks until they die.

Some insects will eat themselves if they're helped to arch their bodies.

Even so, two or three knowledgeable figures have written that irrational beings do not commit suicide; their own conduct or their reactions—sadness and abandonment, aggressive automation, irritation, sexual instinct, fear—can bring about a sudden or slow death, but they don't know they're going to die and are even less capable of knowing how to kill themselves.

At four o'clock I tell Marcela to go take some pictures of the widow Tiflis with her painting and her dog to use with the story, and to ask the señora again about the severed hand and see if she can get anything out of her. The lawyer gave me the runaround and didn't tell me a word about it. "What lawyer?" "I'll tell you about that later. Right now I'm expecting the Candé girl."

At five o'clock the Candé girl hasn't shown up and I'm snoozing on the sofa.

She arrives at six in her school uniform with her books.

I want the portrait and pictures from Europe back, she says. Since Marcela's the one who has them, that will have to wait. I'm about to tell her she'll need to work that out with Marcela and not make me waste my afternoon when I realize she knew perfectly well who had the photos, and that it wasn't me. It must be a pretext for starting a conversation because she has something to tell me.

I probe, going back over what I talked about with her aunt and uncle. I ask her, as I asked them, if it was only Adriana who heard voices, and whether Adriana really did hear voices or only pretended to hear them.

At that point she breaks her attentive silence to correct me.

"They weren't voices."

I pause. All right, they weren't voices. Yet another version. What were they, then?

"Letters."

"Letters?"

"Letters."

"They summoned her in writing to somewhere?"

"They didn't summon her. They told her she had to kill herself."

"They ordered her to kill herself?"

"No. They told her she had to do it, without forcing it on her."

"Why?"

"Because being alive is not worth the trouble."

That's when I turn to face her. "Who thinks that? You?"

Her cold lucidity vacillates for a moment but she recovers immediately. "No. That was what the letters said."

"You wrote the letters?"

"Is that an accusation?"

"No. Nevertheless," I state with a certain discouragement, "at this stage it will be impossible to convince me that your aunt Adriana actually did everything and endured all her brother and two sisters say she did. All they do is try and distract us from the truth, so no one will investigate, or even if someone does investigate, the truth won't come out. They're covering for someone, for you."

"You're mistaken. My mother and my aunts and uncle have all told the truth ... some of it."

"What's the other half? The letters?"

"Yes."

"And if that's the truth and no one's managed to find it out yet, was it necessary for someone to know?"

"Yes, it was necessary."

"To see what happens?"

"To see what happens."

"Why choose me?"

"Because you're determined to know, and when someone does something with passion, the people around him go along with it, even against their will."

"Don't make a speech—" I stop her with a hand gesture, I command her.

I can't believe it.

I'm thinking energetically about a news article, get it out right now, a scoop, but first I have to finish up with the girl here; this dialogue is good material for the series, I should have recorded it; she must have been intimidated and she doesn't intimidate easily. She's still standing there, she's not leaving, she's waiting, waiting for what, she has me tangled up in all of this and it may well be that she never wrote a letter nor was there ever any letter of any kind.

"Who wrote the letters?"

"We never found out."

"Who signed them?"

"They weren't signed."

"Where are they now, in the case file?"

"They disappeared before the police could search the house."

"There can't have been very many people who were in a position to get their hands on them."

"Of course not, only Mamá and I were in the house."

She's challenging me. Now I wonder what she wants. An adventure? What sort of adventure, with me? But I retreat from that idea just in time: What she's trying to do is make me suspect the mother.

"Your mother took the letters?"

"Yes."

"She's the one who wrote them?"

"No, but she knew who it was."

"So the police never heard a word about this, I'm guessing."

"..."

"Will you tell me, once and for all, who it was? Or what you're trying to do besides set more traps for me? What do you want—to destroy your own mother? You hate her that much?"

She waits for my flare-up to subside, then says, "Mamá saved me."

"You're the author of the letters?"

"No."

"Are we starting in on this all over again?"

"My aunt wrote the letters to herself, she did it herself. She'd put them in the mail and then when she read them she'd go pale and be upset for hours and days..."

This is the truth now, I have no doubt. The girl made this statement with vivid emotion, no longer trying to provoke me, her eyes squeezed shut, clenched fists resting on her knees.

Time passes, and after a while hands begin organizing books, fingers run through long hair...

I help her get herself back together, speaking in the voice of a friend. "I still don't know your name, only your family name..."

She tells me, and I call her Emilia, and she feels better.

Then I ask her to think, about me, more or less as she's done up to this point. She asks me how and I tell her I'm only pretending to see things clearly. She understands, she was aware of that. She tells me that seeing things clearly is very difficult. I tell her that what I require from her, what I need her to try to do for me, is help me take one step further. She agrees and I ask her to explain what she meant when she said, "Mamá saved me."

She nods and tells me that Tía Adriana herself would write the letters, to herself, but that she copied her handwriting, Emilia's.

After she leaves, I keep on thinking about Adriana.

There's no longer any doubt; she wanted to go down and to take the girl down with her.

But for a long time—when she pretended to hear voices,

or when she heard them and confided it to her sister, when she wrote letters to herself and after receiving them from the postman did her best to make everyone notice that someone was inciting her to kill herself—she was sending out signals. As if she were letting everyone know. "Help me," "Love me," "Don't leave me alone," "Don't let me die."

Now I, in my turn, abandon Adriana. I give myself over to stillness, like a traveler at rest. I now know Adriana's story, or whatever part of it can be known, its share of reality, its share of fiction and misdirection.

The seductive cohabitation with madness ends there. Emilia has shut it down.

All that remains at the bottom of the glass is one final dreg: Why was terror joined to somber pleasure? (The question no one knows how to answer.)

For my part, I'll go on living. At least provisionally.

From the darkroom, Marcela summons me to come and admire the developed negatives.

She holds them up to the light and I see the "ghosts" of the señora and her nude portrait, but not King.

She asks whether it was important to include him. I say it isn't, though in some incidental way he could be considered significant.

About the hand, she says the señora spoke only one paranoid sentence: "Who knows what ritual the grave defilers may have used it in ..."

Marcela says she's sorry about the dog. "It was impossible, she had him locked up."

"She couldn't let him out?"

"It was a punishment. She said if she let him out too soon he'd develop bad habits."

I observe that she'll be able to take photos again once the dog has served its time.

Marcela tells me that when the señora leaves the apartment, whether for one hour or many, she shuts him up in the bathroom so he doesn't make a mess everywhere.

Absorbed in her work beneath the muted glow of the red light bulb, Marcela stoops over the basins while I hold back in the shadows.

I imagine the enormous dog's terrible imprisonment between four walls of white tiles, the oblivious light slowly expanding across them in all its implacable monotony.

The dog can do nothing but wait (not even expect, or hope: only wait).

He doesn't know that death could end it, nor would he know how to kill himself.

It's a privilege of the absurd human condition, the ability to destroy oneself.

A phone rings in the darkness. Marcela must know what corner of the room it's in.

She leaves the glow of the red lamp and is lost to me.

Her words emerge from somewhere; she says it's for me, a woman. I ask her, in low tones, to rescue me.

I hear her trying to do that, then lose her again.

She reappears to speak low in my ear. She murmurs that the woman is insisting, that it's my sister-in-law. As she says this her body lightly touches mine.

I take her in my arms, draw her to me, and bury my head against her. I don't kiss her, I don't run my hands over her. Something serious begins between us.

"She's waiting," she whispers and guides me over to where, through the receiver, a voice I recognize says, "This afternoon Mauricio had an attack."

Second Part

TRIALS BY ORDEAL AND THE PACT

SUSANA, the wife, shoots out of the little room where my brother is lying as if she'd been fired from a gun, leans against the wall, and gazes upward until only the whites of her eyes are showing.

She makes me nervous but I stifle it and remain firmly in my seat. This is the third of her spectacular exits in the past hour; they do not, in fact, correspond to any change in Mauricio's condition. Susana holds on in there until she can't take another moment of suffering and comes outside to catch her breath.

Then she pulls herself together and goes back in.

I open the door a crack and lean through. Mauricio is asleep under the nurse's care; there's no need for me to go in there or for Susana to stay in there with him, the doctor said so.

I can't do much, only comfort Mamá, who's home watching the grandchildren and is stricken, as was inevitable.

The doctor comes back, recognizes me, and nods without opening his mouth; Susana emerges, no doubt against her will; the door closes behind her and she stays outside. Common sense says I can't help her, and I don't think I should intervene.

A heavyset doctor walks by. Behind him, assiduously gliding along in her rubber shoes, is a nurse who reminds me of something, though I'm not sure whether it's a person. They disappear down a corridor.

A nun says to me, without pausing, "*Buenas noches*. How is she, our patient?" and apart from the confusion, since the patient in question is a he—my brother being, obviously, a man—it strikes me that I haven't seen her here before. But I acknowledge her kindness.

A small woman is pushing a heavy cart: There are covered plates of food on the top shelf and, below, gauze, bandages, tweezers, scissors, disinfectants. Everything has been used, eaten, is going back. She moves very slowly, giving me time to observe her carefully.

The inside of the sanatorium, with its yellow lights, descends into gentle somnolence. The street, too, rests from its automobiles, their noise increasingly rare.

I ponder Mauricio. When he's thinking, he wrinkles up his forehead, maybe because he's making an effort to concentrate. Thinking doesn't make me form wrinkles; I don't believe anything is visible on the outside, in my case. In that respect, we're different. Also with respect to sparrows: I like shooting at them, he doesn't. He was always the one who ate all my candy, which I didn't much care for. He's more muscular than I am; he eats better and used to play sports. He didn't want to die, or so I imagine, we've never spoken about that. If he were to die, Susana would have a hard time of it; they have four children.

Poor Mamá, if anything happens to Mauricio.

My own death, I believe, would be more bearable. She'd get used to it in the end.

The doctor doesn't come back out, he must be examining him, or giving him a shot, or something. Susana is hypnotized by the door, poor thing—her, too. She loves Mauricio and besides that she needs him.

The doctor is taking a long time.

If my brother were to die!

In the early morning, Mauricio is panting, not lucid. Susana, sedated, has fallen asleep on the second bed; I'm on a sofa between them. I've had a wash and the nurse gave me a newspaper. I'm reading the articles with the largest headlines.

Through the window I see people and prefer to watch the children.

Mauricio would protect me from the adults.

In the cellar we had empty cans, oil cans. One day during siesta we banged on them with metal rods until the neighbors stuck their heads over the wall, enraged. We had a lot of fun. Though maybe Mauricio did that for me. Papá had died and Mauricio didn't want to leave me alone, didn't want me to be sad. He gave me his things.

Furthermore—but I only grasped this once I myself was an adult—he understood Mamá's fears better than I did, the risk of helplessness and impoverishment.

Poor Mauricio. I do so little for him, for his children.

Maybe if he makes it and comes home I'd have another chance. I'd take him somewhere and introduce him—"This is my older brother"—in a way that would show him how proud I am that he's always been so good to Mamá and to me.

I look at him.

He could die.

If it weren't for that I might not have realized I love him.

Later Mamá arrives and I wake Susana up. Then the doctor

comes in with a nurse and sends us out. He examines him and is about to leave when my mother, her tears beginning to well up, asks him for hope.

Before answering he looks at her for a moment and I perceive his hesitation. He chooses the truth, saying, cruelly, "Whatever can be done has been done, señora." And he escapes from the pain of another.

"No," says Mamá, "not everything." And she falls to her knees to do what remains to be done: pray.

Susana kneels beside her, desperate with faith. I feel a surge of compassion.

If there were anyone out there to accept the deal, I think I'd say, "My life for Mauricio's"—which, rationally, isn't a bargain that could ever be made. Still, I'd do anything for him.

That afternoon I call the agency from the sanatorium and the boss tells me I don't need to give him any explanations, in these situations family comes first. And by the way, when will I get back to work.

I ask Marcela if there's any news and she tells me she now has pictures of the dog. "Emilia hasn't been back?" "Who?" "The Candé girl." No, she hasn't come back.

There's nothing on my part and nothing in Marcela's voice to bring back the memory of her in my arms.

Later, Mauricio takes a turn for the better.

I insist that Susana go home, get some rest, and spend time with her children. This pleases my brother and during the night—he can't sleep normally yet—we converse.

Strangely, our reconnection happens entirely through childhood memories; the raging river, my blue swim trunks that they stole from me, the two of us as Boy Scouts, Tío Fernando's race car, Papá.

We share memories of him, from the happy times.

Near midday, Susana returns and sends me off—now she's the one giving orders—to bathe, change clothes, have lunch with my mother.

Mauricio is making a double recovery, from illness and from an old injury to his love for his brother.

At home, while Mamá cooks, I let the kids entertain me. Marianita has trapped a sparrow and is keeping it in a cage.

"It's going to die," I tell her.

"It won't die," she says.

"I have experience of these things," I warn, but that doesn't mean much to her; she has experiences of her own. "I gave it food," she explains, as if to remind me reproachfully that whoever has enough to eat will live. That's where she's mistaken.

A few days are enough to erase the unfortunate flare-up of symptoms. The doctor authorizes Mauricio to get out of bed, though not to leave his room. If he takes care of himself —and he will—there will be no fearful aftereffects from the sudden malady.

Mauricio is pious about devotion to one's work, and my desertion of the agency, brief as it's been, weighs him down with guilt, though even as he tries to convince me that he no longer needs me, I can tell how much the thought of dispensing with my steadfast nearness hurts him.

Perhaps he senses what I've been noticing, as well: that our feelings are as pure and solid as they once were, but our time is allocated differently now, which means that once the alarm bells have stopped ringing and we leave this refuge, the disconnections will recur.

But what is this time—I wonder, and the question now has meaning only for me—that I think "we have allocated to us"? Is it the hours of the day? The days of our life? An extremely minor event follows, with its consequences, almost like an answer, to be deciphered.

I've given Mauricio every reassurance that from this afternoon on I'll neglect neither him nor my work.

At midday I notice Mariana's cage has no bird inside and try to get her to tell me why. I simply ask whether it flew away. She shouts, "Bad man!" runs away, and refuses to eat lunch.

To improve the situation, I try to help her understand that she's behaving like the bird; that is, she's upset and won't eat. I make the blunder of threatening: "You'll see what happens if you don't eat."

She weeps and grows desperate. She escapes to the top of the bedroom stairs and won't let us come up, neither me nor her grandmother, under threat of throwing her mother's big mirror on the floor if we so much as try to lay a hand on her.

She puts up strong resistance until Susana rescues her. The girl hurls accusations at me like daggers. I wanted to hit her, I wanted to frighten her to death, I told her she'd die just like the bird.

The mother, who may not have forgotten the slapping I gave to the child of hers that tore up my *Minotauro*, and who's also worried because it's three in the afternoon and the girl hasn't eaten a thing all day, lets herself get carried away in a flood of aversion and condemnation. I foresee that, in her moment, she'll tell Mauricio about every personal defect of mine that will make me look bad.

No matter, I can withdraw.

It was, perhaps, a bit forced. I'd come to see myself, during those days, as if I were clinging to my family's affection, grasping a hook by a single finger with the void beneath me.

I kiss Mamá's forehead, smile to soothe her dismay, since nothing at all has happened, and head off down the sidewalk, calm, lost in thought... At the end of the day, when I'm thinking, it doesn't show on the outside. If other people don't see it, they don't do me any harm.

I remember Papá. I'd like to have him with us, with Mamá and Mauricio.

Then I think about the death of the bird. While it's certainly true that one who eats, lives, it's equally true that one who does not eat does not live, and the imprisoned sparrow did not eat, which led to its not living. And that was the little girl's mistake: She believed that all of us want to live, that it's enough to put the food there in front of us.

As I cross the street, a man comes around the corner, supporting himself against the wall. With his right hand he helps push his right leg forward; once it's solidly planted, he slides the left foot forward—that limb appears to be in good condition—and begins again with the right. Hanging from one shoulder and slung across his torso he has a kind of canvas sack, half open, with provisions sticking out of it: a large, golden loaf of bread, a bunch of vegetables, a package of noodles. He drags his leg along and remains alive; they send him out to buy groceries and, in his way, he feels useful. I turn to follow him with my eyes, he's still walking, down at the far end of the block. Life is tenacious.

Julia's hiding something, prevaricating, but she's grown very tender with me, much more than usual, I'd say.

She alludes to my absence during those days but asks no specific question about the reason for it and I take advantage of that to tell her nothing. I suspect she's getting used to having me leave her on her own for a while and then coming back when I need to, which strikes me as the easiest and most pleasant way. Excessive contact between people produces frictions and irritations. If one individual sees too much of another there's all the more chance of discovering their bad sides.

I say this to Julia and she appears to agree. Nevertheless, she asks what she means to me and without giving it much thought I give her the simplest response I can think of: "Everything." Which is true because I have no one else, though I've tried to. Of course I make no mention of Mamá and Mauricio; in this context they don't count.

I would appear to have left her no way to respond. Unsatisfied, she grows distracted and seems to be deliberating something.

Finally she says something: Why haven't I asked her what I mean to her? And though in fact I have not, I tell her yes, her side of the story interests me, which isn't true though I understand that it's what she wants to hear and that it will bring her into line. She meditates a moment longer, then says: "Everything"—which, in truth, doesn't add anything to the question. But then, giving me a severe and rather odd look, she goes on: "Everything. But *everything*-everything."

She withdraws and disappears for a bit.

She comes back and picks up a chocolate bar and grinds it slowly in her mouth with a somewhat absent air.

She's changed her robe—the one she has on now is showier and more delicate—and she's put on perfume. I don't see

TRIALS BY ORDEAL AND THE PACT · 99

the point but she must have her reasons and she does look better like this.

Suddenly she questions me: Is it at all important to me to know what's going on with her? I tell her that it is and that at some point I was going to ask her.

She then declares that she can no longer endure the shame, and I think this may be in relation to us. However, she reveals that the inspector has suspended her and that this has been the most mortifying episode of her entire existence.

She sobs more than usual, and because I don't know what to do I hand her another chocolate bar, which she delicately rejects, claiming she wouldn't be able to eat it.

I tell myself that in the end, it's all so much theater. I know that.

In the morning, the boss asks whether I'm back. Since an answer would be redundant, I wait for him to say something else.

Then he tells me I shouldn't go all-out on the series, and I don't believe there's any need to respond on that point either.

Apparently it's a bad time for journalism, there aren't so many reliable clients anymore. It wasn't like that before, back when the dailies were devouring our services.

For my part, I see things differently, I tell him. Differently how, he says, and I share my opinion that because of some lapse in the culture, the subject of death is off-limits, which has to do, ultimately, with the fear of death.

He says that isn't true, the papers are all full of death, and I don't insist, though I could tell him about Julia's recent episode at school, which to my mind confirms one aspect of the matter: the vigilant opposition, in family life, to talking to children about death, "don't let them know..." That is, transference, to the children, of the adults' fear.

I don't insist, but say that if I've understood him correctly, we're to suspend our work. Not yet, he answers grouchily, a second circular is going out to the dailies and he has faith, he says. But that's merely a professional courtesy.

I call the sanatorium and Mauricio is taking a stroll out in the garden. All completely normal.

I ask the agency's switchboard operator about Señorita Candé and whether she's called. Señorita Candé has not called.

Bibi is with the Italian. What are they up to, those two?

Marcela is in the lab. I have her bring the photos of the nude and the dog to my desk. It's as if I'd never held her in my arms.

I contact the lawyer. He has the file but can't see me today, it will have to be Monday: Be there without fail.

Julia says over the phone that she's all right and can we see each other at noon; I tell her no because of work and she says all right, nothing more. During her suspension from work she'll have too much time, I think: What will I do? Work is good, it keeps you from thinking too much about yourself; any reprieve—any day off—is fatal. Better if Julia were to take up swimming or some other physical activity.

King, in the photo, reminds me that he interrupted us and I still don't know about Tiflis's face, the señora's version of that story, if she has one. Let's go, I tell Marcela, but she's not enthusiastic. Not that she's out of sorts with me—she answers—it's just...what for. I imagine she's saying this because she's aware there are no clients so it's not worth it for us to go all-out on the series, but she claims she didn't know what was happening in that respect, and I tell her I'm not sure why, maybe because we haven't dangled a glossy, high-priced brochure as bait. She agrees that may be why.

Then I ask her why she said *what for*. She says it wasn't for any special reason. She said *what for*, just like that. And I tell her that, said in that way, it could be a universal *what for*, which sounds rather sad, and Marcela accepts that it may be a universal *what for*, but in no way should it be considered sad, though neither, she acknowledges, is it happy, and that, in any case, is her attitude, and we arrive at Señora Tiflis's house.

Señora Tiflis is already acquainted with the photo. It doesn't horrify her, she saw her husband like that and far worse, after he was exhumed. Someone sent it to her in a stamped envelope, like a letter, she doesn't know who, an enemy of the others in the brotherhood, but also someone who must be a well-informed insider, because it was that same person who alerted her to the mutilation of the body— otherwise how would she ever have found out? The other members must have discovered which one of them sent the letter and the photo because she's waited and waited for further information that would incriminate them, but in vain.

No, until this moment, as we're talking about it, she hadn't noticed the expression or the gaze, though it reminds her of the fierce expression of a painter she doesn't name.

I question her about the hand and she repeats herself: "What ritual did the desecrators use it for?" And asks me whether I've seen the lawyer yet, from which I gather that he must know.

I remember King and ask about him. With her chin, she gestures toward the closed bathroom door.

Marcela, who finds out about cases through her network of contacts, fills me in.

It happened in a slum. Along the blazing, dusty streets there are still spectators, summoned by the police sirens, and by the ambulance siren when it left and when it returned. We got there late.

In the adobe room there's a kind of cloakroom attendant who lets us see the iron bed and the empty medicine bottles on the nightstand. Nothing much there except the fact that this suicide, like so many others, went to bed to kill himself. What does the bed represent to them? Is it an image of their solitude? What does it suggest: deepest intimacy, love, repose, dreamland, a return to the maternal bosom?

He's not dead. He filled his mouth with sleeping pills and swallowed all he could. But for no particular reason his daughter came in just then. She went and got salt and put lots of it in a glass of water, and though the old man twisted away, kicking and moaning, she forced him to drink it. It made him vomit. Before she got married, the daughter was a cleaning woman in a hospital and learned a lot there.

In the hallway, a woman rests her head on a table and weeps softly. I think it's her. The children stand nearby, quiet and solemn, and neighbor women lurk at a distance.

In the hospital, the doctor authorizes a conversation. The old man has agreed to our request and the police officer puts up no opposition, it's a routine case.

The old man says he was tired of being a burden to his family. He lives with his daughter and son-in-law and the couple's children. That morning a niece visited him. As she was leaving, he overheard his daughter telling her, "Everything we have, we spend on medicine."

I ask him whether he's sorry he failed; it's heartless of me but I have to know.

With great joy he says he's not. "I put myself in Jesus Christ's hands," he explains. "If He had planned for me to die, I would have died, but He made my daughter come in and save me at that moment, and that's because He wants me to live."

In the series, I think, this story could be called "God's Judgment."

This episode propels me, without any definite questions in mind, into an armchair across from Bibi. I tell her about it.

It suggests to Bibi that she should prepare a set of notecards on suicide and religious beliefs: the Catholic, Jewish, and Islamic positions on the question. She thinks they may be significant for the series if I decide to digress, if only on a single page, toward the preventive angle.

I say, "All right, but there must also be secular thinking about it. If some thinker without any particular religious bent ever took up the matter, I mean."

"A theory of suicide for the rest of us," Bibi says ironically. "'Suicide is...' 'Thou shalt not kill thyself because...'"

"There are two sides," I clarify. "'Thou shalt not kill thyself because...' and 'Thou must kill thyself because...' Or without any because."

I sacrifice my love of pugilism to the need to placate Julia, but this, too, she turns against me. She says the matches always came first and she sees no reason for that to change. I admit that I have made that point in the past, but perhaps I was mistaken, maybe it's not the best way for me to let off steam.

She goes on defending the boxing at which point I suggest we go to the fights together. She replies that she's still a teacher, despite everything, and I agree that she's right and I shouldn't have invited her.

Then she insists I go alone, if I'm so interested, and all right then. I give in.

I arrive in time to see the headline match but there's no atmosphere, either that or I'm not in the spirit of the evening because I got there so late.

Afterward I head for a late show, some random movie, there's no sci-fi playing anywhere.

When I wake up Mauricio is back home and Mamá tells me to go up and see him, that he won't come down yet.

He looks good, though there are circles under his eyes or maybe he's pale from many days of being indoors. I can't say he's the same with me as we were in the sanatorium, but I understand. He's come home a little nervous, almost distracted, as if he were embarrassed to have caused so much heartache, as if this weren't his home.

Next I go down in search of the newspapers. I go through the supplements, then have a look at the news.

Yesterday, prisoners in Oberá, Misiones, almost all of them charged with homicide or theft, rioted in an obvious attempt to escape.

When a police inspector became the target of their aggression, an officer, to protect him, ordered his guard dog to attack them. At that moment a prison guard closed off the corridor and the enraged animal turned against the officer and bit his arms.

After a judge intervened, the riot was shut down and the insurrectionists handed over their clubs and other blunt weapons.

It came out afterward that they'd asked, through the judge, to be provided with mattresses, to be allowed to practice their respective cults or religions, to receive some magazines, and to be allowed visits from family members.

I analyze the situation, what they're asking for, what they've had to do in order to ask for it . . . The absurdity of it gets me down.

At lunchtime Mauricio stays in the bedroom; his wife carries the plates upstairs.

I imagine he's avoiding being at the table between the two factions. Susana and her daughter refuse to speak to me, and I reciprocate. That, I admit, would be somewhat uncomfortable for him. Mamá isn't happy either, but what can I do for her.

I sleep all afternoon; I may have eaten too much. We had a special meal to celebrate Mauricio's return.

That night I see Julia.

She's still sharp and hostile. If I don't speak, we're both mute.

In fact, I'm getting a little bored. I ask whether something's wrong and I think she throws me an angry look. She exclaims "Is something wrong!" and visibly contains herself.

I refrain from inquiring further, which seems the more prudent course. But she doesn't accept that either and asks why I don't even speak to her. Normally she's more sensible than this.

We spend another moment like that and then she says, "*Hombre*," but as an insult. I let it go, she's been dealing with a lot.

Then she puts aside the rancor and addresses me formally. She says she's still young and there's no reason she should waste her future. I acknowledge this and she throws in my face that there are lots of men out there. I understand and tell her we have plenty of time and shouldn't make decisions only out of wounded self-esteem. She claims that never—and by now I know her well enough or should know her well enough to know this—does she make hasty decisions, and that she's thought it all out very carefully.

I fall silent a while longer and she remains impatient, pointing out to me that we've said everything already.

Since I'm growing distracted and starting to think about other things that don't have much to do with Julia or any of this, I tell her, "All right, I'm leaving now," and she says "*Buenas noches*," which can also serve as a greeting between two enemies who treat each other with strained politeness.

In light of all that, and the fact that she neither softens nor apologizes, I leave.

On Monday Mamá wakes me up with black coffee and asks whether I slept in because I don't have anything to do. I become aware that my head hurts quite a bit. I ask the time and it's eleven in the morning, there's the alarm clock, I didn't hear it when it went off but now its noisy ticktock is bothering me.

I tell her I'm going back to sleep for a while more, and no, I'm not hungry, I'll eat something when I get up.

After she closes the door I lie on my back, head on the pillow, looking at the ceiling bathed in glowing light. I realize I have nothing to think about and notice the headache again, it must be because of the nightmares. I dreamed I was walking around naked.

I soon fall back to sleep and would appear to have rested well because I don't get up until after two o'clock and then with a good appetite and a strong desire to bathe.

Suddenly I remember the appointment that afternoon with the lawyer.

I pass by the agency. I don't find Marcela or Bibi, but there's an envelope from her; she's feeding me tidbits of the promised information.

Fundamental Catholic principle: God alone giveth and taketh away.

Old Testament and New Testament: Do not expressly condemn suicide. / General (& erroneous) conjecture: It wasn't necessary, for in biblical times almost no one committed suicide. / Cases in Scripture: Samson, Saul, and very few others.

Commandment broadly invoked: "Thou shalt not kill." Considered to include suicide / Saint Augustine: Thou shalt not kill man, neither another nor yourself.

Another argument from Saint Augustine: Given

that no law permits anyone to kill on their own authority, suicide is homicide.

Position of the church—Council of Arles, Anno Domini 452: Suicide is a crime; it can only result from possession by the devil. Council of Prague, AD 563: Suicides will not be honored at mass with any commemoration, the singing of psalms will not accompany their bodies to the tomb.

Saint Thomas, interpreted by Sciacca: "He does not properly love himself who puts himself voluntarily to death, for inasmuch as he can consider himself master of the life God has given him, he rebels against the will of his Lord and Father, commits a mortal sin, and deprives himself of eternal salvation."

I reach the lawyer's office just as night is falling—better, that way there won't be any litigants around. He leaves me alone for a while with the legal documents, which I go over and which fill me in on a great deal, which he then repeats in his own words once we reach the spoken part of the meeting.

According to Señora Tiflis's complaint, her husband was affiliated with a secret society, of a spiritualist nature. They practiced ancient forms of worship and maintained a vacation camp on the banks of a faraway lake.

"All very expensive, according to the señora," says the lawyer, "but not to the leaders of the clan, only to the naive adepts, like her husband, who went bankrupt funding big-game hunting excursions and other pretentious activities that served, basically, as the brotherhood's rituals against death, which consisted essentially in killing something, in this case, animals. Fortunately."

The camp does exist, he affirms; there's a map of its location in the dossier. It was raided.

"We searched it," he gets ahead of himself. "Although, the Tiflis case aside, it's really only a summer resort with a sumptuous lodge, a kind of exclusive club for millionaires. No women, no degenerates, but that place is fortified like a military base. I thought about arresting them for weapons possession, to pave the way for a charge of unlawful association. However, they'd foreseen that and produced a license."

The owners? "An association, people without much status —perhaps that's partly the reason none of it came out in the papers—wholesalers, importers, most of them with surnames reminiscent of the Caspian Sea, Omar Khayyám, and *The Thousand and One Nights*. The administrator's name is Jorasán —the widow says he's the one in charge. But this Jorasán doesn't actually own any of it. Very clever, no doubt about that. Not one detail out of order. Everything perfectly legal."

"And the hand?"

"The widow's account fits in perfectly with all the rest. And if a single piece of evidence proving what she says were ever to turn up, we'd have to bury her in jail for the cover-up. It would come to light that for years she helped her husband hide his activities. She only started making a fuss when he was cleaned out entirely and she realized she'd been left with nothing, practically in the street."

The woman may have wasted the lawyer's time and compromised his professional reputation; the display of rancor seemed natural, all the more so given that she wasn't there to hear it. And since none of that matters to me in the slightest, I draw him back to the question.

"I understand. But—the hand?"

"Yes, I'm getting there. I was saying that if it's all something more than a madwoman's ravings, she knows a great deal. For a guy who belonged to a secret society, this Juan Tiflis was quite a blabbermouth. He seems to have told her all about everything."

"He told her all about every imaginary embellishment he made to a few trivial events," it occurs to me to reply, and the lawyer gazes at me attentively. "Loading the rifle would become a ritual; firing it at a deer, an exorcism."

"That may be," the lawyer muses. "It's an interesting hypothesis. The way the widow tells things, it was a bit more than mere fantasy, but, my dear señor, what difference does that make to a dreamer? And this Juan Tiflis was a dreamer who dreamed all the more peacefully because he had a remedy at the ready for the moment when he woke up. Shooting himself, which is what he did."

I nod in agreement and the lawyer, encouraged, goes on. "The basic element, in any case, coheres: the struggle against death. These are individuals of advanced age. They don't acknowledge that, strictly speaking, they'll soon be dead, says the widow, but they know themselves to be at the threshold of old age and they know old age is punished with death. Pay attention to that perspective—'is punished.'"

I say it's not unrealistic and the lawyer is amused. "You see it that way, too?" he reproaches, and points out that they, at least, are possessed by atavisms. "In the primitive societies of the ancient world—the Troglodytae, Thracians, Heruli, Celts—the old were a hindrance and understood this. Or, with astute promises and pressures, the young made them understand it. The Visigoths used the Rock of the Forefathers and the inhabitants of Kea, an island in the Cyclades, drank hemlock during a celebration in their honor. I've had to do quite a bit of research, señor, to comprehend the widow and move ahead with this case."

I tell him, in support of his information, that in the novel *The Top of the World* an Eskimo man and his wife abandon her mother in a frozen wasteland where a bear will eat her, and the old woman puts up no resistance. I share my opinion that this is an extremely barbarous custom, which, if we're to believe the novelist, has been maintained into the present.

The lawyer agrees and I see we're getting along very well.

He says that, in fact, Tiflis's secret brotherhood aspired to save themselves from being eaten by the bear and that, "though more as metaphor, this also occurs in more developed and ethical societies, though in ways that appear more civilized."

He argues, "Look, the universal practice is to make people retire, that is, remove them from their position. Their body and soul are habituated to work and when they're unable to practice their habit they die. It's as if they were being cheated by a mirage: the promise of no longer working."

I interrupt to say that one works, in part, in order to reach a point where one will not work, that not working is also good and at a certain age one can work no longer.

"You see?" he turns on me. "'One can work no longer': old age cannot. But if you maintain"—he's gathering new energy as he speaks—"that a magnate, a businessman, one of the world's powerful men, doesn't have to withdraw or retire if he doesn't want to, I will answer you, *amigo mío*, that there are other, more subtle ways of excluding him and he's well aware of that; at the company they keep moving him into honorary positions and he stops being an executive; at home, the children or the younger wife take his place and lovingly deprive him of his authority."

I can't say for sure that the lawyer is a charlatan but he does talk too much, and he's starting to wear me out. I ask, once again, about the hand.

"Yes, I'm getting there," he promises again. In fact, it's clear he was digressing because he needs a few seconds to concentrate and regroup his thoughts.

"Tiflis's secret society"—he insists on calling it that—"may or may not have a motto, but there is certainly a motto it could have. Always on condition—I must stipulate—that we take the señora's story seriously. That motto would be: 'Do not accept death.' Understand?"

"Yes."

"I'd go further: Do not accept death at any price, in any form, under any circumstances. Got that? Are we coming along?"

"Yes."

"So, if the motto is 'Do not accept death,' then what has the brother who took his own life done? Why, he's violated the principle expressed in the motto, fallen into infamy, turned himself into a criminal."

He looks at me, his bright, expectant eyes clamoring for my admiration. "Just as we were trying to demonstrate," I think, to spare him having to say the words.

He goes on, victorious. "There's more. What punishment can there be for this reprobate? Opprobrium for his corpse. What type of opprobrium? Mutilation. Of what? A hand. Which hand? Why, the hand that raised the weapon in the aim of destroying all that is most sacred—life—and delivering it over to the enemy, death."

I find his line of reasoning coherent, and his conclusion is respectably deft. Even so, I would have wearied of the whole story if it weren't for his vibrant oratorical style, which of course was entirely out of place. The two of us are alone in his office and could have understood each other clearly even if we spoke in low voices and in the simplest terms.

This appears to have been his final flourish and he now considers his statement to have concluded, though I have a strong urge to fire him up again. I don't think it's inappropriate to point out that his argument ultimately supports the accusations made by Tiflis's widow.

He contemplates me, much moved, grasps my hands paternally, and condescends to explain. "My dear señor, such is the magnificent edifice which a great lawyer can erect, even upon the flimsy foundation of a demented woman's obsessions. I invite you to dine with me."

The invitation comes without a transition, amid the rush of his words, their necessary conclusion.

During dinner he starts in again with his animosity toward the señora. "I think, even though he married her, she was no more to him than a body to bring him pleasure—remember, she's a former model—and that his other, purer life was at the camp, beside the lake. He wasn't going to let her in on that by talking about it over the dinner table or confiding anything during pillow talk. If there was a secret part of Tiflis's life, it was what he didn't give her. He killed himself. What a guy, right?"

And his eyes try to wrest confirmation from me. "He was quite a guy, yes, he was. Because he killed himself."

I don't respond.

The afternoon flows slowly toward twilight.

I've been idly strolling around for hours, with last night's story, the lawyer's, in my head.

Convinced that I have now found my path forward, and that it passes through the agency, I've come in, but went straight to my office. My next step is resolved upon and nevertheless I give myself a respite, taking a momentary break from my thoughts to peruse with pleasure Bibi's second report on the moral and religious attitudes of various faiths.

Position of Judaism: adverse to suicide. Biblical basis for this cited by the rabbis: "For thy blood and thy life I will exact acknowledgment; I will exact it from every beast and from every man."

Basis invoked by al-Kirksani, the Karaite: "Thou shalt not kill." (He acknowledges that some claim this commandment only prohibits killing another person.)

Basis of the Jewish attitude, summarized by Reines: "Suicide is condemned because of the dignity of mankind and the conviction that life is always worth living."

Parallelism. Kant wrote: "Suicide violates the categorical imperative, for it annihilates the moral subject, and offends against personal dignity out of the selfish desire to escape from an unpleasant life."

Attitudes of other religions:

Brahmanism and Buddhism. Tolerate and occasionally celebrate it.

Belief in reincarnation makes it more acceptable to the adept.

Nineteenth century: emergence in Buddhist India of the "suttee," suicide of widows, often under indirect coercion from society.

Islam: Condemns it.

Muhammad: "No man ever dies except by the will of Allah, and in accordance with the book that fixes the term of his life." (Quran, sura 3, verse 145)

Marcela comes in, indolent, and takes up a spot on the sofa.

I let her know that I've been pondering the direction of the Tiflis case and believe I've now located the primary witness. I'm about to approach him. He's unaware of his role in the matter. It will all come as a surprise to him, and to her, too, to Marcela.

Marcela pays me no attention, she seems to have gone wandering out through the window.

I look at her legs and say, seriously and with absolute sincerity, "I'd like to be in the darkroom with you right now."

I didn't think she was paying attention but she queries, in a careless tone, "Doesn't it strike you that you're being somewhat impetuous."

I say yes, I do realize I'm somewhat impetuous, but that's what I would like, to be with her.

She doesn't answer or do anything.

A few moments later I tell her the workday is over and invite her out for a drink. She makes no objection.

In the bar, she'd rather have a sandwich and a soft drink and I tell her very quickly that I was with someone but it's all over now. I also say—though there's no need, the atmosphere is cool and peaceful and we don't have anything else to do—that it happened last night and I feel a bit strange right now because evening is approaching and I don't have anywhere to go.

She asks if we had children and I tell her she couldn't, which is not the whole truth.

She stays silent for a while, and I start thinking about nothing. But with Marcela I don't get bored.

When she finishes the sandwich, she takes a gulp from her drink, wipes her mouth with a napkin, and opens her bag. She extracts a manila envelope, shakes out a number of photos, and leaves them lying there on the table between my glass and hers.

I shuffle them around. I'm in all of them. Me, looking ridiculous; me, deep in thought; me, sleeping on the sofa with my left arm, resting on its elbow, making a V; a little bit of me, in profile; and from every other angle, Bibi. The back of my neck, a silhouette, a trick photo with my nose, the dog, and the nude portrait, me in winter, me before the series, me before the series.

I'm amused and her smile is full of goodwill.

I ask her, "What shall we do?" and she asks me, "What's to be done?" and I can't tell whether that's a negative or an expression of resignation.

I say I wish I were like her, and this makes her curious. "What am I like? No, really, how do you see me?"

I tell her, "Unaffected and unselfish."

She has no vanity, I think, and is not displeased by my answer. Instead, she explains, "It's because I'm going to die."

She says it in a fairly straightforward way and it doesn't surprise me. I remember other women, when we were getting started, saying the same thing.

I ask what's wrong, and she must think I've imagined she's suffering from some sort of incurable ailment—which is possible: cancer can affect even young people and especially women—because she clarifies, "No, it isn't that I'm sick."

She says this with a lot of feeling, very differently from the way she generally speaks, as if she pitied me and were trying to convince me there's nothing to be upset about.

It's the same thing I've pondered. I ask if she'll go with me someplace where we can be alone.

She says she'd like to but doesn't think she can.

I ask her whether she's ever done it.

She answers that she was married.

It occurs to me to ask whether she's interested in men.

She puts her finger on the heap of photographs on the table, every one of them featuring me, and says, Do you think I was taking pictures of a jasmine flower?

In that case why not, I argue, and she answers that it's because of what she told me before.

"What?"

"That."

"That you're going to die? I assume everyone's going to die."

"This is not 'like everyone.' I'm going to help things along a bit."

I say "Ah..." and feel a wing flapping inside me. But not for her, for me.

It passes, I think of Marcela and find her abandoned to her thoughts, until she repeats that she'd like to, and I persist with my why not then, and she pays no attention but asks whether I have many reasons to live.

I tell her I don't but she could become one, which visibly annoys her and she tells me there's no need to flatter her.

I realize I've been playing the seductive womanizer when, in fact, with Marcela something will become possible only if there's an intelligent understanding between us. I feel as if I know her well enough for that now, and that's the type of relationship that interests me.

I say all this to her, trying to be clear.

She says that yes, something like that is what she wants,

too, which is why, before anything happens, she'd like me to tell her whether I would take my own life along with her.

She's very serene and is obviously leaving me plenty of time so I don't blurt out whatever first occurs to me.

I notice she's asked me if I would kill myself with her, not if I would kill myself for her, and I think that's because Marcela is different from other women.

Why does it surprise me to find myself confronted, here, now, with the question that continually besieges me? It must be because it's coming out of someone else's mouth. I feel my anxiety starting up again and I want to see things clearly. "And why would we do that, Marcela?"

"No particular reason…Is there a need for one? Life makes no sense."

I understand, or think I understand, though vaguely, that these would not be my reasons.

"Marcela, even without sense, life offers a lot of things I like."

"Me too. But fundamentally it's not worth it."

And she suggests we change the subject.

I go along with her on that, although I would like her to know I feel cornered.

A certain unease has set in, and when the waiter comes by—we've been there for a long time and have spent very little on our two drinks—Marcela says we can leave.

No one can seriously discuss their own death with another person, I think.

The next morning there's a case and Marcela is already there, as always.

They let us in, though without the camera, and the individual is still lying in the place where he did it. He dressed as well as he could for the occasion, and I catch a whiff of cologne.

He used the double bed. Next to it is another one, also quite wide. It may be for the children, who weren't there when he took the poison.

The judge handles us with discreet kindness.

He invites me to notice: The man put the portraits of the little boy and little girl on the pillow, no doubt so as to look at them, or so they would be with him to the end. But, he says, what he should have done was beg their forgiveness for the very idea, and abandon it.

Since the judge permits, we follow the whole procedure.

Over the morgue door a clock ticks. Around the face is an inscription: "Every hour passes by, except the last one." That doesn't resonate with me but only reminds me of the clocks in all-night restaurants that say, "Every hour is a good time to eat." I say so to Marcela and she thinks it's funny, but this is no place for laughter.

Then they authorize us to go inside. The doctor is at work on the suicide. The scalpel has made a deep opening in the corpse. Marcela whispers that the man must not have given much thought to the autopsy or he wouldn't have worn cologne or his blue suit.

The motionless bumps on the room's stone floor repeat into the distance. I wonder if that's what Marcela is giving her attention to.

It's nearly two o'clock, and Marcela drops me off near a restaurant but continues on because she'd rather have a shower before lunch.

It's very hot and I have my siesta at home where everyone's resting.

I bathe, pick out my lightest suit, and head back to the agency.

Marcela calls me into the darkroom; she's blowing up the shots she took that morning with the miniature camera.

Other photographers are in there and I can't do much, but I do caress her two or three times in the darkness.

We have dinner together and Marcela is wearing a different dress, very light—I think it's made of gauze.

Afterward I leave with her and we are carnal.

Marcela gets up early; she has different habits and cuts off my sleep.

We go to the agency in the Citroën and she heads for her darkroom. She'll load the cameras with film, just in case.

I negotiate with the boss, ask him for sixty minutes of his undivided attention, that is, behind closed doors with no one else present.

"Is it urgent?" he inquires, and I say, "Yes and no." He specifies, "If yes, then now, right now this moment, and if no, then later on in the afternoon." Always energetic, concrete, and efficient, he makes me feel small, and I'm suddenly overcome with the feeling that what I want to talk to him about is pointless. "This afternoon, or some other day, it doesn't matter," I reply. He moves on.

Bibi lifts me out of my abandonment. "You're making me work," she says, her tone somewhere between complaint and contentment, and she places the third section of her report in my hands.

(In fact, the fervor Bibi brings to this subject is beginning to make me wonder.)

REJECTERS

Pythagoras, Plato, Aristotle, Dante, Luther, Calvin, Shakespeare, Spinoza, Napoleon...

Albert Camus: "From the absurd, I derive three consequences: my rebellion, my freedom, my passion. Through no more than the play of consciousness, I transform what was an invitation to death into a rule for living: and I reject suicide."

Kant: "Suicide is abominable because God forbids it. God forbids it because it is abominable."

Jaime Balmes: "The fundamental reason for the immorality of suicide is that man thereby disturbs the natural order, destroying a thing over which he has no dominion. We merely have usufruct of life, we do not own it; it has been granted to us to eat of the fruits of the tree but with suicide we take the liberty of cutting it down."

ACCEPTERS

Confucius, Buddha, Diogenes, Seneca, Montaigne, Voltaire, Rousseau, Hegel, Nietzsche...

Hegesias of Cyrene, in his philosophical school in Alexandria, encouraged suicide among his disciples. With some success.

The Stoics were defenders of man's free will and prescribed suicide as the remedy to any woe.

Schopenhauer: "There is nothing in the world to which every man has a more unassailable title than to his own life and person."

Nietzsche: "One should live in such a way that one may have the will to die at the right time." "Suicide as ordinary mode of death, with the suicide the new pride of mankind; he fixes the moment of his own death and makes a celebration out of dying." "The thought of suicide is a great consolation..." "Let there be no regret; suicide is quicker."

EXONERATIONS

For freedom (Kant), honor (the church fathers), many for ideas, the nation, religion, etc. John Donne, Dean of St. Paul's, denied that suicide is sinful in every case and asked for charity and compassion (*Biathanatos*, 1644).

COUNTERPOINTS

1

David Hume: It is contrary to the law of God, for according to religious beliefs everything is foreseen by Him and nothing happens except by His will. (Exegesis of *On Suicide* by Reines.)

The Tosafists, before Hume: While everything is predisposed by Heaven, it is not written that anyone must end his own life in water or in fire.

2

Suicide is contrary to natural law since nothing in nature destroys itself. (Josephus, in the *History of the War of the Jews Against the Romans*.)

Suicide is not contrary to nature; it gives free rein to the individual's own discernment of how to dispose of his life. (Hume, in his essay on suicide.)

*

The meeting with the boss. He orders coffee and mineral water. He orders that we be left alone.

He appears to think I'm there to speak to him about some routine new matter, because he says, "First I want take advantage of seeing you to let you know not to work too hard on the series." I remind him that he already told me that and he begs my pardon: "Oh, yes. I have so much on my mind!" That's true. If I were in his place I'd accomplish far less and bungle far more. But we're different.

He hasn't yet asked for a complete report, though that's his system; on a certain day he'll say I have to finish up and I'll know that the free flying is over and I have to lock myself in and pay for my vagabonding by writing the entire series within a week, maximum.

This time, on my own initiative, and because I have a specific goal in mind, I tell him everything. The students— "I am going to kill myself," "Me, too"—and the elderly father, made suicidal by love, but who drifted off to sleep instead; the police, who aren't cooperating, but Piel Blanca is, and also wants to get married: What do you think of her? Then Tío Eduardo, the voices, Emilia...the nude portrait, the dog, the lawyer, the hand.

A lovely narrative chaos, since I have a full hour at my disposal. He glances at his watch but stays interested. When I'm done, he tells me, "It might work," which I take for an initial sign of approval. Even so, he laments, "It won't be any use, there are no buyers, at this point we have only one magazine, in Caracas, four-color, paying in dollars, naturally. We need at least two more and between fifteen and twenty newspapers. At least."

I ask whether the series is canceled. He says not yet. I say, then let's get on with it. He looks at his watch and I tell him, "I'm finishing up here. The only thing left is the primary witness. That's you."

He doesn't take this for a joke, which it isn't. On the contrary it seems to bother him. For, I tell him, he has work to do, too.

The photographs, of Tiflis and Adriana Pizarro—was he the one who took them? Of course not. Then who was it? He told me, when he placed all of it in my hands, that they came to him from a respectable professional. Well, that respectable professional learned of the mutilation of the corpse before either the widow or the police did. He's the one who instigated the investigation and warned the wife, and before that, to provoke both anxiety and trust, and to obsess her, he sent her the photo. What was his aim? To destroy the secret society, if it even exists? Was he a traitor to the clan? That may be, and it may not be. He's not the one who claimed that Tiflis's brotherhood was responsible, that was the wife. Why she's doing that, I can't imagine. But there is someone out there mutilating corpses, and he, the sender of the photos, knows or suspects who it is, and wants to eliminate that person without showing his face, so he incites the widow and she does precisely what he expected: She goes running to the police. "If you tell me who it is," I say to the boss, "the story has an ending."

"Before writing the ending," the boss requests, not the least bit dazzled by my thesis, "explain one contradiction to me. A corpse is exhumed with part of the body missing, and a millionaire's club is raided, and all the while not a single newspaper gets wind of it—"

"Or does get wind of it but doesn't publish."

"That may be. Around here, at least, we didn't know anything about it. But I'm focused on a different angle. Hear me out. Three, four, or five months after the case was closed, somebody puts three photographs at the disposition of an international press agency: One is of Juan Tiflis, whose death may entangle many people. Let's ask ourselves, why didn't the agitator who doesn't show his face alert the press when it all happened, and why is he doing it now?"

The boss's mediocre grasp of the situation is making me feel quite astute. "He got the widow all wound up so people would start poking around and there would be an investigation, right?"

"It certainly looks that way. That may be right."

"That's it. The investigation happened, but it failed. And now, what's he doing? He's winding up a new pair of puppets: you and me."

He's lost but doesn't give up. "I think we have to go back to where it all started. And it did not start with the particular case of Juan Tiflis and his posthumous mutilation, that's no more than a detective story we can use to our advantage. What I asked you for is something different: the mystery of people who kill themselves. We have our starting point: those two faces."

The mystery of those who kill themselves! He might as well be asking me to resolve the mystery of death itself in ten six-hundred-word installments, each illustrated with five color photos, for one magazine in Haiti and two others in Senegal and Norway.

I defend myself. "You gave me two faces. I'm supposed to decipher them, right? And how can I do that without their stories? There are only two people who could help and they aren't coming back to tell me what they saw or felt during those moments. And they are the people whose faces those are, as you know."

He indulges me and his whole physiognomy takes on an expression of reverence. "That's so true . . . there's no coming back."

He's stuck on the most obvious point. But I understand him; anyone, at any moment, can remember that he will die and measure the significance of what he will lose—life— because "there's no coming back," "there's no coming back to life."

Nevertheless, his fear of death, like almost everyone's, comes and then goes. He says, "I gave you three photos—"

I don't know how he intends to finish the sentence but allow myself to interrupt. "Forgive me, someone gave you three photos, but did so to conceal his true motive: Only one of them mattered, the one of Juan Tiflis. By chance, there happened to be two, Tiflis and the Pizarro woman, with open eyes, which is uncommon among suicides, and that aspect of the matter threw us off track. Am I wrong?"

He reflects on this in silence. Then he says, "That may be the case. But I believe you're mistaken on an important point."

" . . . "

"Someone manipulated the widow, I agree, and managed to get an investigation launched. Then he provoked me, so the case would be reopened, to see if journalism could achieve what the law hadn't managed to. Is that what you think?"

"Yes."

"And this person, who addressed himself to the widow, and then addressed himself to me: What is he trying to do?"

"See to it that someone is punished."

"Precisely. And who is this someone? He himself."

He beams as if he'd won a chess match in a single move. He hasn't won yet. I attack a position I think is weak. "If the first investigation focused on the wrong things, since the señora didn't accuse the author of the letters but the brotherhood, or if the señora's intuition was correct and the responsible party was a member of the secret society but the investigation was mishandled, why didn't our agitator reorient her with further evidence? Why isn't he helping us right now by sending us a letter every week?"

"Because he is the guilty party and if the police inquiry had succeeded or if our investigation succeeds, he'll be found out and punished."

"And that's not what he wants?"

"When he wants it, he sends the photos and the letter about the hand. When he doesn't want it, he keeps silent. You see? He wants it and he doesn't want it. He wants the guilty party to be punished, he's suffering from guilt and denounces himself because he gives in to the dictates of his own conscience, but then he notices that what will be punished is his own body, and his mind and body shy away from that."

Now I'm the one who says, "That may be the case," and, in the same breath, I'm the one who argues, "But you would know that because you're a very well-placed witness: Only you know who gave you the photos."

He denies this with a smile and a movement of the head that says, "Give it up, my friend."

I make my final point. "You said, 'a respectable professional.'"

"I did say that." He shrugs. "But they came by mail."

I say nothing.

That's it then. The matter is concluded.

"What do I do?" I ask.

"As long as I haven't given you the signal to stop, go ahead with the series."

I have Marcela without ever having courted her. I point that out because I think it's good to see things clearly, and ask her, in turn, to be clear with me.

She feels it wasn't necessary for me to court her, that I am the way I am and she understands me.

It occurs to me that I haven't ever spoken a word of tenderness to her, either. Marcela confirms that I haven't, up to this point, not a word.

I explain that if I don't, it's because I wouldn't feel comfortable doing it. She can understand that and forgives me.

Nevertheless, so everything will be clear, she should know that at one point in the past I did say those words. I tell her I was once in love.

I was still a student, and she had a charm that was cloudless and pure. We were both seventeen, the age of loving well, and we loved each other elegantly.

Even so, I distanced myself from her, suddenly. It was my intention to go back some day but I neglected to tell her so.

I was far away and sent no word. Then I did go back to find her. She'd married someone else.

I withdrew even further to protect her from any feeling of remorse: If I erased myself, she would never come to realize that she had no faith in me.

I say that I can't know whether things would have worked out with her because I believe, or at least now I believe, that you marry a certain person and then that person changes, and most often this new person no longer interests you, or not in the same way. Or you think you're marrying someone, but you're only marrying that person's youth, and youth doesn't last.

Marcela agrees, and I tell her that this person continues, for me, to be that other, original person because I've never seen her again. I remember her as she was at seventeen.

Marcela tells me that I still love her. I acknowledge that may be, but maintain that it would disturb me if she, in turn, were still to love me, since I am another person, and not a better one, either inside or out, than when I was seventeen.

But in any case, this is an inadequate conversation because it is melancholy, even if I'm making Marcela aware that, in general, everything you believe to be fundamentally good for yourself is not possible. And that goes, as well, for my relationship with her, which is fundamentally good yet nevertheless has a time limit, I don't know what it is, though I'm sure she's established it.

Marcela falls silent and since we're very close to each other in the darkness our bodies knot together in passion and afterward I tell her that whatever she wants to do with me I'll do, but again she doesn't answer, which humiliates me.

It's Friday, the third Friday of the month. But that doesn't matter, I pay no attention.

Except I'm unavoidably annoyed because I don't manage to meet the person who was supposed to be waiting for me, and then an importuner cuts me off and traps me, and I flee from another notorious busybody, stumbling over people covered in fleas to clamber onto a bus that takes me away but the bus is a lethal cauldron or gas chamber, so I seek some air in a plaza and the cool waters of the fountain but there, from a bench, I'm assailed by the lamentable debris of a woman.

I pull myself together and seek beauty. It's there, it exists, it's all around. It abounds, almost. The slender bodies and high-held heads of youth, a face, a pair of eyes, the colors that spill down through the air onto people, a mature forehead, a delicate hand in flight... they emerge, pass by... and are lost in the torrent of human ugliness.

Some days are like that.

Evening has settled onto the neighborhood.

A man lying in his hammock along the sidewalk undoubtedly got up very early and has worked all day; he yawns. It sounds like a lion or a solitary wolf, I'm not sure which. His dog looks up at him but is used to it. I'm not, and I stop. Over there, a group of ladies are observing him discreetly from the corner of their eyes, they huddle closer to one another—they're walking arm in arm—and quicken their step.

We ape men exist, too, that is known: horse men, amphibious men, men whose earlobes are unattached or free.

All of us, upon reaching a certain age, have the right to retire.

In a film or novel, if the protagonist kills himself, the story ends.

If he kills himself at the start, it's because we'll go backward, and the story will be told after a leap into the past.

*

If I kill myself, I don't only kill myself, I kill my death wish, too.

I'd like to kill others, also, but no one in particular. Some because they're cruel swine who make the world an ugly place, and King, who's suffering.

My death wish is also a wish to kill others.

I can't kill them, at least not all of them. But *I can* do away with all of them: If I do away with myself, they'll no longer exist for me.

I go home in the morning and Mamá doesn't ask me anything, though of course she's sad and jealous because she realizes what's happening.

She wants to know whether I'll have lunch with them and I say I can't, I have to work. Have I had breakfast then? I say I haven't, which isn't the truth but I do it to make her happy. She serves me in the kitchen and I ask about Mauricio and he's working and eating, doing very well, the scare is over.

Then I shut myself in my room.

I search for the letter. I put it in an envelope to preserve it from everything. It's from her.

I find it. Her lovely handwriting. I read it, and her tender delicacy flows through it, even amid the prudent complaint, the muted alarm of the confusion I caused when I left her without giving any reason.

I set fire to it in the ashtray. Before that I caress it with the tips of my fingers.

There's also the wooden letter opener that came by mail without any indication of who it was from. I've kept it all this while in case it was from her. I never used it. I think I should have used it, as she may have wished, to open a path through my readings. I'll have to start doing that now, at last. I choose an uncut book called *La veneración*; I believe the title is appropriate.

Papá's watch, with its worn silver plate... Still soft to the touch, just as before.

The gold Parker, which will be left to Mauricio.

I make out the companionable little noise of the alarm clock, audible from the night table; I haven't been around, so it's undoubtedly Mamá who's been winding it.

I open a drawer, and my skin recognizes the little handle, polished smooth by my pulling on it since I was a child. Every piece of furniture bears the traces of my touch, they've shaped themselves to my habits, and my eyes have adapted to seeing them where they are.

A memory takes me down to a corner of the courtyard.

When I was a boy, for my entertainment, Papá tied a handful of balloons to a nail in the wall with string. Within a few days some of them had popped, and others had lost their air and become tiny and wrinkled. Someone took the balloons away, but the string stayed for a long time, I noticed it there years later, because it was under the eave and neither sun nor rain damaged it.

I don't think I've remembered it since and don't imagine it could possibly still be there. Still I want to see for myself.

I have no trouble locating that part of the wall and yes, the old bit of string certainly has disappeared, but the nail, under innumerable layers of whitewash, remains. Perhaps my father put it there with his own hands.

I greet my mother, she sighs, and, no doubt alluding to the new woman in my life whom she doesn't know, says, "May it be for the best, *hijo*."

When I see Marcela she asks where I was. "Saying good-bye to some things," I tell her, and she understands.

One night I tell Marcela about the girl in the window.

They were demolishing the old school and its spacious courtyards, behind my house. At the back of the lot, a wide, horizontal apartment building went up. Little by little people moved in.

A young woman leaned out of one of the windows and stayed there, contemplating the evening.

I had the idea of waving at her, and she responded in kind.

We saw each other every evening, the girl in the window of the apartment building, me on the terrace of my house.

We didn't signal each other in any other way. I thought that at some point I would go looking for her.

Between the two buildings was an empty lot, and a building went in there which blocked my view of the window. I didn't see her again.

Marcela asks me what else happened with that girl and I tell her nothing, nothing else.

The morning's reading matter:

A couple was found dead in a hotel.
The receptionist heard two gunshots on a high floor.
. . . accompanied by a retinue of police . . . room 501, 5th floor, 22 year-old female, unmarried; 41-year-old male, married . . .

Both of the deceased presented bullet wounds to the right temple. According to the experts, the man shot his companion, then took his own life.

Two letters were found next to the bodies. Their contents have not been revealed but there is presumed to have been a suicide pact between the pair.

That night we're alone, in the dark, in each other's arms. I ask her, "When?" (Our pact has no date.)

She doesn't answer.

I don't insist, I wait. It's Monday.

Bibi invites us both to her house. Her mother shares the table with us and the home-cooked meal tastes of hospitality.

I seem to detect an awareness of our situation, I don't know if Marcela confides in Bibi.

In any case, there are no questions or insinuations, nor is there the toast that, even without being made, is suggested when a final bottle of bubbly is served in special glasses.

Which makes things easier because it frees us from questions about the future.

The mother declares, "You young people can stay up late, but not me, I'm an old lady." Then her resolute discretion wavers and she smiles at us in all her goodness, takes Marcela's and my hands into hers, tenderly exclaims "*Hijos míos,*" and goes no further but contains herself and heads off to bed.

We didn't look into each other's eyes for a few moments, the three of us left at the table, and then, with the coffee, the moment passed and we were on to something else.

We put on a record, two records, three records, we look at one another and it's a bit empty in here: What shall we do.

Bibi laments that we're not journalists in Italy, where

playboys and playgirls from aristocratic families would drive us in roaring automobiles to their grandfather's castle, its high stairways lined with sculptures, and we'd all dine by candlelight, clad in evening wear.

"Then we'd wander off, two by two, among the salons and gardens."

"Or we'd play a sinister, fatal game."

"Or we'd do all of the above in front of a camera, filmed by Fellini or some other director, Signor Whatever, and the intimacy of the crimson bedroom would repeat itself in the gaze of two thousand pairs of eyes, for hundreds of nights, in hundreds of theaters, and so on for all eternity."

Bibi declares that she would like that, anyway, and proposes we put on a show. I think she's doing this to be polite to her guests, though it really isn't necessary.

She explains that for me—so I can write it—she's come up with a spectacle that she's already made notes on, which could be called *Daily Life in* . . .

"Where?"

"In many places, many eras."

She quickly gets excited, drags us to her room, throws us onto her bed, and tells us to study the papers she hands us.

I read. Marcela reads. Bibi waits.

These all seem like Bibi's inventions, she's made a satire out of everyday characters and deliberately selected fragments of literary and dramatic history, including Shakespeare.

I stop reading and so does Marcela. Bibi's been watching us and understands. She says, "I know, I know: It won't work."

"We could still try," Marcela says to encourage her.

"No," Bibi admits, "we're not drunk enough and there's nothing suggestive or atmospheric about this house. My bedroom is my bedroom."

"But I," Marcela rises resolutely to her feet and, playing along, transforms herself into a whispering, venerated crone, "I'm in Athens and I observe to my neighbor, 'That Patroclides was a courageous man, he took his own life without even asking permission from the Senate...'"

Now it's my turn, and I step straight out of ancient Rome to declaim energetically, "The law must exercise greater rigor in forbidding the act of suicide. Perverse habit, even the slaves are hanging themselves now. At this rate, who will cultivate my lands?"

Marcela, a prince's wife in medieval Lorraine, applauds the Roman lord. "A prudent and necessary remedy. Good heavens, what damage the servants' pretension to dispose of their own lives does to us. How can we allow it, how can we tolerate it?"

I go further back in time: I'm Zeno, the Stoic. I fall, hit my hand, fracture a thumb. I stare in indignation at the ground and reproach it. "'I'm coming to you now, earth! Why do you call me?" and lift my fingers to my neck to strangle myself.

Delighted, Bibi assumes a dramatic attitude, picks up a serpent, and clutches it to her bosom.

CLEOPATRA: Come, enchantress of death! With thy pointed tongue untie this knot of my life! Be angry, poor poisonous creature, and finish quick!

Enter Marcela.

CHARMIAN: "Oh, eastern star!

CLEOPATRA: Peace, peace! (*Indicates the asp with her eyes.*) Dost thou not see my baby at my breast? That sucks the nurse asleep? (*Dies.*)

*

A long silence has ensued. Bibi is tactfully putting out the lights, except a single nightlight that illuminates one side of my face. I emerge from the stillness as Beethoven, confessing to a friend, "I'd have committed suicide long ago if I hadn't read somewhere that it's a sin to part from life voluntarily so long as one can still do a good deed. Life is so beautiful, but for me it is forever poisoned."

A very gentle moment, and then this erupts:

HAMLET: Who would fardels bear, to grunt and sweat under a weary life, but that the dread of something after death, the undiscovered country from whose bourn no traveler returns, puzzles the will and makes us rather bear those ills we have than fly to others that we know not of? Thus conscience does make cowards of us all.

From the shadows, someone says:

AN ORDINARY VOICE: Suicide is for cowards!

And I say:

KIERKEGAARD: Agreed, it is cowardice, but it is a cowardice that demands a great deal of valor.

Bibi switches on the lights; the smiles each of us finds on the others' faces demand to be seen. We celebrate our delight in the philosopher's sound reasoning and restrained eloquence.

Immediately we find ourselves with Marcela in a workers' café, circa 1930. Bibi goes past, dancing with a fellow who is economically superior to the place's ambience. Marcela crucifies her. "That one over there … she'd do anything for money and for luxury, she'd even cut herself with a Gillette."

But Bibi prefers Hadrian's Rome and proclaims the emperor's newest decree to his armies: "The soldier who attempts suicide will be punished." By what? "By death."

For my part, I must die in the preceding century. I am Nero, my enemies have come to sacrifice me, and my friends surround me as I demand, "Kill yourself someone, now, in my presence, to give me courage." No, they don't help me. I'll have to do it on my own. "What a death for so great an artist!" I drive the dagger into my throat. Epaphroditus joins his strength to mine and we drive it in.

Dead—according to the note by Suetonius that Bibi has passed me—with my eyes exaggeratedly wide open, I inspire fear and horror in the others. I remember the photographs of Juan Tiflis and the Pizarro woman, and refrain from interpreting this part.

In any case, Bibi, who's helped me out with the maneuver of slashing the dagger through my throat, is satisfied and is applauding.

In short, we manage to endure the night.

I've completed another day and am sharing the night's rest with Marcela.

Marcela asks if I've had other experiences of love or only the one, and I wonder out loud whether she's joking.

She demonstrates very seriously that she isn't joking, and I talk to her about the girl on the tram, I don't know why I tell her about that, I've never told anyone before, not even my brother, these stories have always stayed inside me.

It was a while ago, of course, there are no trams now. I was coming back from somewhere with a photographer. I noticed a young woman looking over at us and we were drawn to each other, what caught her attention may have been my companion's camera.

I spoke to her, she was on her own and had a white lace collar on over her dress.

I think we liked each other quite a bit. We agreed to meet

again the next evening at a certain time and place: a street corner. I didn't give her my name, she didn't give me hers: Why bother with that when we would be together, perhaps forever, starting the next day.

I got off the tram with the photographer, we had work to do, and the girl rode on.

The afternoon I was supposed to see her, it rained. A little rain wasn't going to stop us, but then the flooding started and it was impossible to go anywhere.

Marcela asks whether I didn't go back to that same corner on another day, and I say no, because we hadn't agreed to meet at any other time.

These interludes of conversation during our nights together are very pleasant; Marcela listens to me and isn't jealous.

I think about Mamá.

She has Mauricio, she has the kids.

Maybe I gave Mauricio back to her. I said, when he was sick, "My life for his." He's come back to life, and now I have to pay up. It would strengthen my resolve to persuade myself that that's the case.

I never stop pondering this bargain. Who would accept it? Who could require payment from me? Might Marcela be that individual's agent, his emissary?

My answer is a smile.

I think about Mamá.

Grief doesn't kill anyone. Who knows.

I have to choose between Mamá, poor woman, and myself.

Or someone has to choose for me. Not Marcela. I can't ask her to do that.

Maybe not someone but something.

Something supernatural like a roll of the dice, the dice that tumble along until they stop, leaving face up the side with the number no one could predict.

Dice aren't supernatural. Is gambling supernatural? Is chance?

I wonder if the supernatural has its laws.

I propose to Marcela that we play "a supernatural game" and ask whether she believes in the supernatural.

She doesn't think there's any point in talking about her beliefs, she believes the same as everyone else.

I tell her I think she's different. She replies that she isn't.

The supernatural game consists of dreaming. If the two people who've agreed to the wager dream the same thing, on the same night, the game has been successful and the dream has one meaning, and if they don't dream the same thing then its meaning is different.

Naturally, since it's so hard to create a coincidence, you have to try and promote it, which is done by having the two spend the hours before sleep together, share the same meal, observe and handle things common to both or that one and the other can give equal attention to. It's best, I explain to her finally, if the players are a man and a woman, and if they sleep together.

She asks whether I've ever played it before. I haven't and explain that in fact I've just invented it and am trying to establish the rules.

To tell the truth, in our case, the coincidence-promoting prelude is managed without further deliberation, and the rest, when bedtime arrives, is normal.

When our heads are on the pillow Marcela asks what we're betting, and I tell her each of us is betting whatever seems right, since it's not a matter of defeating the other person but of *betting against oneself*. This seems to appeal to her and we agree on another newly created rule: that there's no need for one player to tell the other what's at stake.

My reasoning is that if I bet my dream won't be the same as Marcela's, it will be very easy to be right, and I'll thereby deprive the game of courage and substance. The improbable outcome is that we'll both have the same dream. And if everything inside me is driving me to kill myself, I can only be curious about a sign that tells me not to take my life.

Therefore I bet that if Marcela dreams something that resembles what I dream, the sign will be no. And *no* would mean not to do it.

Upon awakening, Marcela tells me her dream:

A group of strong, voracious men were eating a stew. She and I stayed in a corner. We were inside a stone hut up in the mountains.

Then I wasn't there and they wanted to take advantage of her, which did not happen.

They'd thrown us out into the snow and we had to move forward. If we stopped, they would fire their Mausers.

It was snowing and we found shelter in an abandoned mine shaft. A few yards inside, in the darkness, a wild beast's yellow eyes filled us with terror.

We couldn't escape: Snow had blocked the mouth of the cave.

The beast was moving, it was crouched atop a pile of wood, the logs clattered as they fell, knocking against each other.

The storm was over and we were walking across the snow, which was infinite.

We had to keep moving forward because the hungry beast was following us, yet we stumbled, fell, overcome with sleep. We were awoken by an animal's tongue, licking us, and it wasn't a wild beast but a humble domestic dog that was scared and wanted our company.

A cold sun appeared, not even yellow, but enough to melt a little snow, and a blue pool was forming.

We went on walking, we were comforted now.

Marcela doesn't remember any more than that, and I've lost our supernatural game.

I tell her it doesn't matter whether she remembers the rest of it, her dream is already packed with detail.

She asks what I think and I say I think that if she wants to interpret the meaning, it's very clear: salvation and hope.

She wonders, "Salvation from what? Hope for what?"

I consider that quite clear, too: Salvation from fear.

I tell her it's strange that she dreamed about snow and I didn't.

She wants to know why and I say I promised Mamá I'd take her to the snow.

She asks if we had the same dream and I say we didn't, I dreamed I was walking around naked.

Today's Friday, the anniversary of the day I was born, thirty-three years ago.

I catch Marcela studying me, once or twice, then averting her eyes. She asks whether something's wrong.

I tell her no, but that it's a special day.

I don't feel like saying why it's a special day nor does she display any interest in knowing why.

I board a bus that leaves me at the cemetery, now's the best time, later on the sun will be exhausting.

Papá's niche looks well-tended, no doubt Mamá came to tidy it up yesterday and today she'll come visit with all the rest of them.

"Your wife and sons will not forget you," the plaque's inscription promises.

From the tiny portrait, Papá looks out, his gaze alert and penetrating.

As he sat for the photographer, could he have imagined that the lively glance he directed toward the camera would watch us forever from behind glass?

The glass reflects me and it occurs to me that my inner image has left my body, which looks no different on the outside, and wants to slip inside the niche. But it hasn't gone beyond the glass, it's still there on the surface, an intermediate zone between inside and outside.

I become aware that contemplation of the tomb has absorbed me.

I react, wondering what will happen, and I also remember Marcela.

I think I'm going to go soon, and first I have to say something to him, I've always spoken to him, when I was small I'd ask for things. I can't think of what to ask for this time so I try to soothe him. "Soon Mamá will come, with Mauricio. They'll bring fresh flowers," and before I turn toward the exit we gaze at each other, Papá and I, through the glass.

As I'm boarding the bus I bump into an elderly lady and put her at some risk of falling. A few people spring to her aid with an exaggerated air of protection and I hear murmurs of reproach and hostility. I could beg her pardon, but there's no reason to, I did it accidentally, unintentionally, as everyone should assume.

When the lady is settled in her seat—more than one has

been offered her—she turns toward me with some piteous words.

I stare at her, not sternly but in sadness, and she abandons her question.

Possessed by the demon of summer, flies buzz around me and brush against my skin, and the world is harsh and violent.

The house is quiet, as if it were night, but the familiar souls are absent.

I go upstairs and pause in front of the open door of Mamá's bedroom, as fresh and neat as the bedroom of a teenage girl. The sun shines through pink curtains and the green branch of a tree shelters the window from outside.

I go to my bedroom, which has few charms but watches over the end of all my daytimes and welcomes and supports my times for rest.

The canary's trilling pulls me back from the quiet life of objects and invites me to the courtyard, where my mother's hands bring vitality to various planters filled with greenery whose names she knows and whose diseases she foresees and cures.

I pause for a moment in front of the nail, then go back to the pleasant shade of the house where all indicators appear to confirm Mamá's certainty that today's lunch will unite her with both her sons.

Later she comes back and they are all there, Tía Constanza, too, and I can see they've all dressed in their best for the visit to the cemetery, maybe they also went to church.

Mamá kisses my forehead and Tía Constanza my cheeks,

and both express their hope that my birthday be a happy one, that's how they put it and they're sincere.

My brother is trailing behind them and seems to be suffering from the heat, he's taking off his jacket and tie, and while that's understandable given the sun and all the rest, I sense he's also waiting to talk to me.

Mamá heads for the stairs and I go to Mauricio and ask about his health and he says "*Bien, bien,*" though I can see he's preoccupied. Soon enough, when we're alone in the living room, he tells me successively, and far too heatedly, that I forgot that it's been twenty-five years today, and that for me, feelings don't matter, Mamá is suffering, I've lost all notion of honor and respect and...

I want to defend myself and raise a hand to contain him, make him stop talking, but he misinterprets the move and slaps my hand away. Then immediately he aims his left hand at my face, and I push it away which further inflames him.

He throws himself at me, he's the heavier one, I could move aside, dodge him, but I don't because he's Mauricio.

He punches me in the head, one-two, then again in the solar plexus, and I fall and he stands above me, waiting. It hurts terribly and I'm in a daze, though I've managed to grasp that my older brother is punishing me for something.

And Mamá is clamoring that we're both her sons, but that doesn't have much effect, and the light is very bright and up above the children are watching all of it.

I need to be alone, and I go off and lose myself among the crowded sidewalks of the city center.

But the noise of walking feet and the reflection of the sun on the pavement drive me further: pain, stupor, bewilderment, and exhaustion require that I rest. I think of a café, a plaza, a park; instead I go into the City Bank and settle down on a leather bench along a wall, no one pays the slightest attention to me as they cash checks, make payments, exchange dollars, send wires, transfer funds.

After a time I grow distracted and begin observing the ladies who are acquiring booklets of traveler's checks. I select one of them, she's young and delicate, and accompany her from Stockholm to Rome, two days on a train with no other passengers on board because every journey is its own mythology.

I manage to gain access to a telephone and dial the agency's number.

The switchboard operator recognizes my voice and says, "I'll put you through to the boss, he's been looking for you," but I say "No, no" to stop her in her tracks.

Then she asks, "Who, then?" whom do I wish to speak to, and I ask whether I've had a call from a certain Señorita Emilia Candé, and she informs me that I have not, she asks her fellow operator who confirms, no. I ask whether it's possible she may have called yesterday, or the day before, or the day before that, at some point. The operator answers that she never called.

I go back out into the street, and the everyday world is passing by, or a bit worse than everyday, there's a hot wind blowing.

I'm hungry, I buy myself an ice and retreat to the refrigeration of a movie house to watch *Fahrenheit 451* twice, it's premiering.

By the time I leave it's night, that's what I wanted.

The wind keeps up, it goes *uuuuuh*, here it's encanyoned by the buildings, in the mountains it's encanyoned by the canyons.

I have a beer and a toasted ham-and-cheese sandwich. I needed that.

I think about Mauricio. He must be desperate, he's a person who suffers from remorse. I could phone him and tell him to forget about it, that on my side of things it's completely forgotten, I'll see you tomorrow, it doesn't hurt at all anymore. (Tomorrow... ?)

I think about her letter, the one I set fire to in the ashtray. I have no other, she never wrote me again, I can understand that, I didn't write her back. I might like to have a portrait of her from back then. I'd like to see her... as she was.

It's 9:20, and nothing's happened.

It hypnotizes me, the train that shakes the high iron railings and seems to throw this bridge out across space like a balcony, that takes in all the air as it passes and leaves a vacuum in its wake that pulls me down...

When it goes into the curve my whole being veers with it and I'm going to fall over the edge to my death, danger! Red light!

... Someone is waving an emergency lantern, down there on the ground between the tracks.

The train is far away, the iron rails silent.

Beneath this bridge the trains fly past and fly past again.

*

Some human beings fall from up there, from this bridge.

If you're religious, it must be harder to go through with it than if you aren't. You think, "It won't end with this; afterward there's hell."

Marcela says, "You're back." I say, "It's been a special day."

She thinks she's guessed, some trace must be left on my face. "You had to get into a fistfight with someone." I think about that, and say, "No."

"Have you eaten?"

I say no, but I'd rather have a shower first.

She sits across from me—she doesn't eat, she already had dinner—and watches me eat, which bothers me though I don't say so.

She says, "I wanted you to come back."

That's reasonable and I have no response.

Then I ask whether she has a record player, any records. She says she doesn't, what for.

Julia did have records.

I remember I never said goodbye to Julia, and what if it were to happen tonight . . .

Marcela wants to know whether I'm getting tired of her. I tell her I'm not the least bit tired of her, that's never happened to me with her.

It's the truth and it pleases her to hear it, and immediately she suggests we go to bed.

I find that strange, but the day is over.

*

The hot wind has us under siege. She wanted to open the windows but had to close them again.

It's stifling in here and fatigue is grinding me to a fine powder.

I tell her I'll sleep naked. Marcela has no problem with that, I've done it before.

I take another shower. I come back fresher and lie down beside her. She wants me to look at her, I was looking at the ceiling. I look at her and say, "You haven't taken your clothes off, how can you stand it?" According to her, she can stand it.

Marcela strokes one of my arms and soon we're kissing.

Afterward she stays in her universe, barely making her presence felt, and I'm already a little sleepy but she says my name and asks me if there's something I never succeeded in doing however much I wanted to.

I ask when, and she says, "At any moment in your life."

I say, "Direct movies, like Bergman."

"You'd like to be Ingmar Bergman?"

I say, "Well..."

She says nothing more and I'm starting to fade, but I still have the presence of mind to ask what she would have wanted to be.

I think she answers, in a very gentle voice, "A passenger on an airplane that never lands," and a wave of sleep engulfs me.

I come out of the night's lethargy to find myself in daylight.

The calm is flawless, the sun still inoffensive.

Marcela has opened a window and left me there, a pagan who sleeps without modesty or shame.

I feel my body abandoned to softness and drowsing, nothing troubling its inner rhythms, the silent rush of blood.

There's no tension, maybe because I slept well. Sleeping is good and I was lulled to sleep by Mauricio, who's my brother.

Or maybe it's other things that I've been unburdened of.

The punches I took still hurt a little, when I think about it.

Poor Mauricio, I can't fail to take care of him. I'll tell him, "It's the three of us, with Mamá, just like always. Are you happy now?" And he'll nod in agreement.

It's after eight, and yesterday the boss was looking for me.

Marcela doesn't come in, no doubt she's making the coffee and toast we like to have.

I slip my feet into slippers and wrap myself in the sheet. I'll tell her, "I'm a Greek, from long ago," and see her smile.

I find her in the living room. She's lying on the sofa and she's dead.

I make certain of that, then have to go back into the bedroom. I sit on the edge of the bed. After a time, I get up and lower the blinds, it's better like that, in semidarkness.

I go back to where Marcela still is.

The head is thrown back, the eyelids half open. I can see the eyes but she's lost her gaze.

No somber pleasure alters the shape of her mouth; it only looks as if she were wanting water, still feeling that thirst, even now.

I make an effort to remember her dream about the mountain, the supernatural game, and what I told her: that it meant salvation from fear, obviously.

I sit down in front of her, bow my head, and weep.

Then I realize the tightness is already gone.

From below, from the inner courtyard, rises a little girl's voice. She sings an innocent song and I listen, captivated. She stops singing and the seduction of the moment slowly dissolves.

I reread the paper that Marcela left the bottle of pills on top of, like a paperweight, and that I've been clutching in my fist. "Don't do it, I beg you."

I read it again. Then another time, and another.

It's eleven o'clock in the morning.

I have to report this, which will be troublesome.

I have to put some clothes on because I'm naked.

Utterly naked.

That's how we're born.

TRANSLATOR'S AFTERWORD

"HETEROPESSIMISM," a term coined in 2019 by Asa Seresin, meaning, roughly, a pessimistic view of heterosexual norms, usefully names the mood of many works created long before the word existed. For example, *El mundo de la mujer* (*The World of Woman*), a short documentary filmed at the 1972 Femimundo trade fair in Buenos Aires, expresses what we might now call peak heteropessimism. Leggy, hollow-eyed gamines with zero body fat and elaborate bouffant hairdos mince down the showroom runway past bewildered children, embittered-looking mothers and grandmothers, harried husbands, and dour businessmen. On the soundtrack a man reading excerpts from the Femimundo catalogue alternates with a woman reading from Disney's *Cinderella* and a "Guide for ascertaining what every man's ideal is in a woman . . ." The man says, "You live in a universe that thinks only of you, in a country whose most powerful companies work only for you." The woman says, "You must be romantic, undemanding, generous, easygoing, happy, and casual, while always maintaining a bit of mystery and never letting him see you're tired."

The film's director, the great María Luisa Bemberg, co-founded the Unión Feminista Argentina. Soon after the film's release, "Isabelita" Perón, the former dancer who'd become both First Lady and vice president of Argentina in the 1973 elections, assumed the presidency after the death of her husband, Juan Péron. Isabelita's ascent to power was no victory for women, or for humanity. During her administration, the country was primarily run by José López Rega, a sinister figure with twin passions for black magic and fascism. By 1976, when the world's first woman president was ousted in a military coup, the state terror campaign known as the "Dirty War" was well underway.

The Suicides, first published in 1969, conveys a hetero-pessimism much like that of Bemberg's film, though the novel sees it through a male lens. The nameless single man who tells the story works at a news agency, goes to boxing matches every Saturday, loves watching sci-fi movies like Jean-Luc Godard's *Alphaville* (1965) and Ugo Gregoretti's *Omicron* (1963), and collects the Buenos Aires sci-fi magazine *Minotauro*, published from 1964 to 1968. He's been shaped by writers like Isaac Asimov and Arthur C. Clarke, who fill *Minotauro*'s pages in translation, and probably also by another Argentine periodical of the day, *Adán* (*Adam*), which would have been the perfect client for the illustrated series of articles on the eros of suicide that he's cooking up at work. *Adán* marketed its *Playboy*-like hedonism as resistance to the strict Catholicism of the military dictatorship that seized Argentina's government in 1966, the year it launched. *The Suicides*, written and set during that dictatorship, barely alludes to any local or national politics or system of government. There's only the criminal justice system: the police, the judiciary, the prisons.

The narrator, a self-proclaimed "normal man," ogles every young woman he runs across, at work or in the street. A photographer coworker he thinks must be his own age is too old to interest him, while a 17-year-old schoolgirl, the niece of one of the suicides he's investigating, is the female whose intelligence he most respects and whom he most yearns to hear from. Although he almost never thinks about the changing gender expectations for women that are happening all around him, they do affect him. He lives in his childhood home with his doting mother, his brother, and his brother's wife and four children, while several of the women he sleeps with, or tries to sleep with, live alone. All the women he pursues are, like him, employed. Unlike him, some own cars, and they drive him around. His housewife sister-in-law does not emulate his mother's pure self-abnegation but complains about him, even quarrels with him. And he's dimly aware that the schoolgirl who draws his attention is off-limits.

He demonstrates glancing knowledge of Margaret Mead's work on the social construction of gender in her 1935 *Sex and Temperament in Three Primitive Societies* (published in Spanish in Buenos Aires in 1947), a comparative study of three Melanesian societies: the warlike Mundugamor, the pacifist Arapesh, and the Chambri, among whom, Mead claimed, women were dominant. He's also aware that there are alternatives to heterosexuality, suggesting to a policeman that two teenage boys who've perished in a murder-suicide may have been involved in an unhappy love affair. Yet his perception of gender as destiny remains ironclad.

The gender whose destiny concerns him is his own. He's preoccupied with manhood, what has become of it, and his own place within the lineage that extends from his fearsome paternal grandfather to his suicide father to himself and his brother. A news item about a man who committed arson to give his volunteer fire brigade a chance to hone its skills makes him reflect on the existential absurdity of firemen with no fires to put out. The dossier of types of suicide his colleague Bibi, a.k.a. the Card Catalogue, prepares for him includes the case of a warrior who kills himself for want of a war. But does the problem really lie with the modern world's restrictions on masculinity? Bibi later brings up the Roman emperor Hadrian's decree that the penalty for a soldier who attempts suicide is execution. Then there's King, the "chained maniac of a dog" that Juan Tiflis, one of the suicides under investigation, left to his widow, who keeps the large mastiff locked in a bathroom where he spends all day howling. You don't have to be human to be denied the life evolution destined you for.

One of the narrator's girlfriends describes a dream she had about an animal that turned out to be her father and devoured her. Then she found herself in a mud pit attacked by a wild boar that turned out to be the narrator. Her dream reminds him of some ideas vaguely recollected from Freud, though he doesn't believe they are applicable to her. He explains that he would know what her dream meant with greater certainty if he or any other man had dreamed it. His own dream life seems somewhat impoverished, even to him. He mainly dreams he's walking around naked.

Twice, though, he dreams of a woman who is his "professor of English." This comes out of the blue, almost as if it weren't the character's dream at all, but the novel's: a dream of its own translation, fifty-six years after it was published, thirty-nine years after its author's death. But of course that's the story I, the woman translating the novel into English, would tell myself.

Antonio Di Benedetto (1922–86) never said anything about having written a trilogy. But his work has a strange porousness; it welcomes the possibility of being acted upon by history. In 1999, the Argentine novelist Juan José Saer proposed reading three of Di Benedetto's novels as a Trilogy of Expectation that begins with *Zama* (1956) and *The Silentiary* (1964) and concludes with *The Suicides* (1969). Saer's proposition has proven convincing to many, though the central characters, time periods, and literary styles of the three works are quite different. While *Zama* takes some of its prose style and tone from the period it's set in and, as Roberto Bolaño noted, from Kafka, the two later novels also respond to the French nouveau roman and the existentialism *The Suicides* wryly alludes to in its epigraph from Camus. Even so, the novels' parallel structures, situations, themes, and chronological development speak to each other, enrich each other. Over the past decade, the three have several times been published as a single volume.

Don Diego de Zama narrates the first book, whose three sections are titled 1790, 1794, and 1799—and are perhaps echoed in the enigmatic title of Bolaño's *2666*. Don Diego has no notion of the enormous changes to come just beyond that time frame. Napoleon's occupation of Spain in 1808 would weaken the Spanish Empire's grasp on South America and lead to successful wars of independence across the continent. *Zama*'s readers do know that, however, and can read the novel as an ironic prelude to that future. Closer in time, *The Silentiary,* which takes place in a vague period just after World War II, also offers its own strange prehistory of the present into which it was published in 1964.

The aspiration to offer a history of the future poses a greater challenge to the trilogy's final volume. While its protagonist loves dystopian sci-fi—the primary elsewhere, besides death, he's able to imagine escaping to—*The Suicides* is emphatically set in the present of its own writing and publication, something it underscores with multiple references to contemporary novels and films, and even the date of someone's suicidal leap from the Eiffel Tower on March 12, 1967.

The sense of immediacy is heightened by the third novel's several parallels to its author's biography. Unlike the earlier selves in *Zama* and *The Silentiary*, the narrator of *The Suicides* is a professional writer, a journalist, as was Antonio Di Benedetto, who wrote novels, short stories, and screenplays on the side and made his living working for *Los Andes,* a local newspaper in his native Mendoza. When Di Benedetto was eleven years old, his father died very suddenly. He was never entirely sure whether the death was a suicide.

Still, this is not what we would call autofiction. There are significant and substantial differences between author and protagonist. When he wrote *The Suicides*, Di Benedetto was more than a decade older than its central figure and a married man, the father of a daughter, Luci, born in 1961. And his life was moving towards a drama different than anything confronted by this protagonist, though strangely similar to the denouement of *The Silentiary*. On the day of the 1976 coup that deposed Isabelita, Di Benedetto was arrested and held by the state for more than a year, subjected to torture and mock executions. He was never entirely sure why.

All three of the trilogy's novels are narrated by a male protagonist in his midthirties: Christ's age at crucifixion, Dante's *mezzo del cammin*, and Di Benedetto's age when he wrote *Zama*. All three narrators are drawn to an elsewhere that will liberate them from their current circumstances. All three erupt into a fistfight with a male rival at a climactic moment.

Each work reaches a dramatically inconclusive ending. And in each successive volume, the protagonist's access to power has waned. Don Diego de Zama, a high-level official of the Spanish Empire, can transform the lives of underlings at will. Nevertheless, he lives in poverty and frustration, ever conscious of his inferior status as an americano, born in the New World, and seething with thwarted ambition and resentment of the authority exercised by the viceregal governor and distant king.

The nameless hero of *The Silentiary* also feels trapped and powerless, though he exercises near-absolute control over the lives of his mother, wife, and eventual infant son, moving them endlessly from house to house in his personal quest for quiet. He retains some of Zama's belief in his power to alter his situation, working with a newly elected city councilman (a former journalist) to pass a local noise ordinance, and with his electrician cousin to create a jammer that interferes with the neighbors' radios and TV sets. He grows enraged when the councilman-journalist says to him with a laugh "You've thought about killing yourself, haven't you? That way you won't hear any more noise"—so enraged he punches him in the face with a set of keys. His desire to change things for the better leads him to toy with the idea of open warfare against the noise-makers who poison his existence, and in the novel's final pages he's in prison. He emphatically rejects the idea, suggested to him by a dream, that this might be a conscious sacrifice on his part, that he might be deliberately saving his family from himself.

Zama, too, ends with involuntary sacrifice. Rather than executing Don Diego outright, his captor cuts Zama's fingers off, whispering that if he cauterizes the wound in the embers of the campfire he might survive. In Lucrecia Martel's overwhelming 2017 film *Zama*, which does not transfer the novel to the screen but encompasses it, responds to it, sees into the depths beyond it, the Indian Don Diego was told might save him does appear. In the film's final scene, an indigenous child sitting opposite the mutilated Don Diego in a swiftly gliding canoe gazes at him gravely and asks "Do you want to live?"

The novel, however, ends differently. Don Diego sees a blond boy, a figure he's glimpsed several times already, whose age never changes in the course of a decade. This could be an actual rescuer but can also, and perhaps more plausibly, be read as a dying man's final hallucination of his own earlier self.

Don Diego de Zama's dissatisfaction is personal; he wants to improve his own situation. The protagonist of *The Silentiary*, however, may be the "dissatisfied" person that his counterpart in *The Suicides* thinks should be in charge of all governments, the kind of person who "won't resign themselves to anything, who will always demand that everything should be improved." Written and set, like *Zama*, during a period of worldwide political upheaval, *The Suicides* offers only a single glimpse of an active demand for improvement: a prison uprising. The inmates demand mattresses to sleep on, freedom of religion, and the right to receive magazines and visits from family. The narrator, coming across their story in a newspaper, finds it absurd that they've resorted to violence and risked their own lives only to demand so little.

What are his demands? Certainly he wants sex, the "results" he tries to "produce" with several of the women he encounters. Aside from that, he may be enacting the detective novel the silentiary thought about writing, trying to solve a mystery largely of his own invention, something he conjured up out of a couple of superficial coincidences to pander to his boss and create a lurid commodity for the agency to sell. The mystery has some connection to his own life, but the problem of a parent's suicide can't be solved by deductive reasoning. Nor, as he knows full well, can reason resolve the enigma of the facial expressions of people who've just killed themselves.

Like every protagonist in the trilogy, he has a mutinous attitude toward his boss. His two earlier counterparts are tormented by financial anxiety and spend a lot of time pondering intricate accounting schemes; this narrator would like to keep his job but otherwise appears almost devoid of financial anxiety or ambition. The histrionics that accompany several of his romances cause him no anguish but serve only to keep him mildly entertained and, occasionally, sexually slaked. The factors that are causing him to ponder suicide seem to be external: each day brings him closer to his birthday when he will reach the age his father was when he committed suicide—on his birthday. He also toys with the idea that suicide might be genetic; his grandfather boasted about the number of soldiers and suicides in the family. (The one suicide in the book whose motivation is perfectly clear is that of cousin Paolo, who kills himself out of terror of the grandfather, to escape his vengeful patriarchal rule.) Perhaps —why not?—the narrator will enter into a suicide pact. Is he in the grip of a death drive pushing him to do himself in, or is he telling himself a story, building, out of a couple of coincidences, a plot, a theory?

The epigraph to *Zama*—"A las víctimas de la espera," which I've translated as "To the victims of expectation"—gives the posthumously conceived trilogy its title. The two earlier novels revolve around a dissatisfied man's expectation of some improvement in his life. The expectation that permeates the third book is more generalized; it seems to envelop everyone. Adriana, one of the two suicide cases the narrator sets out to investigate, suffers from the madness that afflicts the authors of novels, a sense of "not being one individual: of multiplying herself: she was everyone else." She's gone to great effort to stage her suicide so as to cast blame for it on her young niece. Perhaps the entity she's actually accusing is the implacable march of time that has turned her own earlier self into what she is now. For his part, the narrator blames her family for ignoring her strange behavior, which was, he decides, a plea: "Help me." "Love me." "Don't leave me alone." "Don't let me die."

Adriana was crazy, several observers agree (though Bibi disputes this term), but no one thinks the male suicide Juan Tiflis was mentally unbalanced. He was a dignified elderly gentleman, drawn in by a powerful sect of wealthy death-resisters until he rejected them by killing himself. (The hand later amputated from his corpse is a remote echo of Don Diego's severed fingers.) Tiflis's widow, however—also middle-aged and alone, also done in by time, as the portrait of her younger self that hangs in her tiny apartment shows—is considered a madwoman by her disdainful lawyer. Gender is expectation; every character in *The Suicides* is formed by gender expectation and is a victim of it, some more than others.

The narrator registers only the most general features of the women he pairs off with; one is a schoolteacher, another has very fair skin, etc. (Age is his primary criterion for potential sex partners, but the names of some of the women he lusts after, pale Blanca and the Candé girl—whose family

name derives from candor, Latin for whiteness—are a re-
minder of Don Diego's criterion, which was race.) Marcela,
the journalist's photographer coworker, is particularly difficult for him to perceive. "What am I like?" she asks him.
His response, that she's "unaffected and unselfish" seems to
mean that unlike the other women in his life she is undemanding, easygoing, casual, always maintains a bit of mystery,
never lets him see she's tired. She requires nothing from him.
And she is spectral, shape-shifting. At first unacceptably old,
she suddenly grows young enough. He wonders whether
she's a virgin; she answers that she's divorced. After she shows
him a sheaf of photos she's been taking of him without his
knowledge, even before they started working together, he
wonders whether she's even interested in men. Her sardonic
response—she seems to grasp how little about her he's taking in—is as close as she ever comes to articulating anger.

How must it make her feel when he tells her later that his
fantasy ambition is to direct films, like Ingmar Bergman?
All he's ever seen in her photographs is their subject matter.
He notices nothing, says nothing, about her skill, framing,
composition, texture, use of light, or vision of him, though
she's told him that her ambition is to photograph the aspects
of people they themselves don't see.

Marcela shares her spectral quality with a series of vanished
loves he tells her about: the cloudless, pure girl he fell in love
with when they both were seventeen, and whom he then, in
contemporary parlance, ghosted; the girl he occasionally glimpsed
from a window in the back of his house; the girl he once met
on a tram and never saw again. The blankness of this romantic history connects the Petrarchan ideal of the love object
as distant, inaccessible muse to the TV trope of the "dispos-
able woman," whose relationship with a protagonist allows

her disappearance or death to generate strong emotion without need for much in the way of character development.

When Marcela first mentions her intention to die, it doesn't surprise her new boyfriend; he's heard other women say much the same thing at the beginning of a relationship and takes it for normal female self-drama. When he wakes up one morning to find her dead, he's staggered, then, very quickly, exhilarated. She has sacrificed herself, and he is saved, he tells himself: supreme, naked, Adam in the Garden of Eden, reborn. But is he? Earlier, when his brother suddenly fell gravely ill, he told himself a similar story of rehumanization, redemption, the restoration of brotherly love.

Within the Trilogy of Expectation, Marcela's suicide is prefigured by innumerable previous disappearances. The Guaná and Mbaya peoples, the cacique Nalepelegrá, the enslaved African woman Tora who tells Zama that her body bears the marks of a beating her mother received when she was in utero—they all have vanished by the time the second novel begins, at which point the annihilating colonial project that Don Diego de Zama was part of has been realized beyond anything he could have conceived. The African and indigenous presences in *Zama* are simply not there in the later novels, and act on the protagonists only by their absence, or as the dimmest of echoes. The silentiary hears a Black man's "rasping, velvety voice" in a dream of the year 1830; the journalist working on a series about suicide is vaguely aware of indigenous peoples in remote Melanesia. Both narrators have an only slightly less dim historical awareness of a place neither has ever been, Europe—and, within it, the Old

Country, Italy, where the journalist's grandfather once returned from with a desperate young widow.

In the two latter novels, most of the vast racial and linguistic differences that Don Diego lives within are gone. Entire peoples, cultures, languages, and lifeways have vanished, lost without grief or awareness, as if they'd silently chosen to eliminate themselves, as if no one were responsible, as if they'd never really existed to begin with. Though only Don Diego de Zama is aware of it, all three narrators are colonizers. Yet they feel colonized by their circumstances, experience themselves as the victims of their own and other peoples' expectations, or what the silentiary calls "not-allowing-to-be."

The silent violence and unacknowledged destruction take a toll. Jimena Néspolo, a novelist and critic whose work helped bring Di Benedetto to the central position he now has in Argentine literary culture, wrote me early in the Covid pandemic about how extraordinarily contemporary *The Suicides* is "in this suicidal world of ours." Our present is easy to recognize in a novel whose protagonist gets lost in long threads of disjointed factoids, where the news media exists to generate sensationalist content for profit, where brotherhoods of the wealthy build themselves sumptuous fortresses against death, where the gritty heat grows more intense with every passing day. That its narrator could somehow undergo a genuine transformation in the final moments of *The Suicides* seems as remote and preposterous a possibility as that Don Diego de Zama somehow does survive the severing of all his fingers. But if he's not reborn, what becomes of him, and of us?

OTHER NEW YORK REVIEW CLASSICS

For a complete list of titles, visit www.nyrb.com.